Women would fall at his feet, yet he'd channeled his energy into his children. How cool was that?

He wanted this party for his daughter, and Thea had catered events for both women and men. This man was no different from any other client.

And that was when she recognized the lie.

She liked Scott and that made him different. Which was why she wanted to turn him down flat.

Then she looked head-on into the intensity of his gaze and her stomach did that whole stop, drop and roll thing that had nothing to do with being pregnant.

From another lifetime she remembered falling in love with her husband. The ache inside when they were apart. The sheer giddiness when she saw him. The heart-pounding excitement. The anticipation to be together. Her heart stuttered and her stomach fluttered as it occurred to her that this was very much like what she'd felt long ago.

But that was impossible. She was the caterer, he was the client. And their relationship was—had to be—strictly business.

No matter what sizzled between them.

Dear Reader,

Well, the lazy days of summer are winding to an end, so what better way to celebrate those last long beach afternoons than with a good book? We here at Silhouette Special Edition are always happy to oblige! We begin with *Diamonds and Deceptions* by Marie Ferrarella, the next in our continuity series, THE PARKS EMPIRE. When a mesmerizing man walks into her father's bookstore, sheltered Brooke Moss believes he's her dream come true. But he's about to challenge everything she thought she knew about her own family.

Victoria Pade continues her NORTHBRIDGE NUPTIALS with *Wedding Willies,* in which a runaway bride with an aversion to both small towns and matrimony finds herself falling for both, along with Northbridge's most eligible bachelor! In Patricia Kay's *Man of the Hour,* a woman finds her gratitude to the detective who found her missing child turning quickly to…love. In *Charlie's Angels* by Cheryl St. John, a single father is stymied when his little girl is convinced that finding a new mommy is as simple as having an angel sprinkle him with her "miracle dust"— until he meets the beautiful blonde who drives a rig called "Silver Angel." In *It Takes Three* by Teresa Southwick, a pregnant caterer sets her sights on the handsome single dad who swears his fatherhood days are behind him. Sure they are! And the MEN OF THE CHEROKEE ROSE series by Janis Reams Hudson concludes with *The Cowboy on Her Trail,* in which one night of passion with the man she's always wanted results in a baby on the way. Can marriage be far behind?

Enjoy all six of these wonderful novels, and please do come back next month for six more new selections, only from Silhouette Special Edition.

Gail Chasan
Senior Editor

Please address questions and book requests to:
Silhouette Reader Service
U.S.: 3010 Walden Ave., P.O. Box 1325, Buffalo, NY 14269
Canadian: P.O. Box 609, Fort Erie, Ont. L2A 5X3

It Takes Three

TERESA SOUTHWICK

SPECIAL EDITION™

Published by Silhouette Books

America's Publisher of Contemporary Romance

I dedicate this book to Valerie Florence Pascale and
Emma Maria Pasqualino—two IVF miracles and the
inspiration for this story. Thank you, ladies.

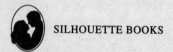

SILHOUETTE BOOKS

ISBN 0-373-24631-5

IT TAKES THREE

Visit Silhouette Books at www.eHarlequin.com

Printed in U.S.A.

Books by Teresa Southwick

TERESA SOUTHWICK

lives in Southern California with her hero husband who is more than happy to share with her the male point of view. An avid fan of romance novels, she is delighted to be living out her dream of writing for Silhouette Books.

THEA BELL'S FAVORITE FAMILY RECIPE

1 egg—liberally laced with hope
1 sperm—bountiful with unfulfilled promise
Simmer with hormones and put in a warm place

Add 1 seasoned father of two
Sprinkle generously with attraction
(Keep hot, but do not permit to boil)
Combine two cups of conflict
A dollop of determination
Then fold in a liter of love

After nine months, remove promptly. Baby makes three
for a happy family.

Chapter One

"Someone's been cooking in my kitchen."

Staring at the beautiful stranger in front of his stove, Scott Matthews figured he'd hit a low point even for him. His life was reduced to a culinary caper of *Goldilocks and the Three Bears*. Except the woman wasn't a blonde. She had hair like brown silk, eyes warm as hot cocoa and was *not* sleeping in his bed.

"Who are you and what are you doing here?" he asked, annoyed that the sleeping-in-his-bed thought sent a shaft of heat through him.

She wielded a spatula like a conductor's baton. "Who are *you?*" she demanded.

"I live here."

"You're Kendra's father?"

"Scott Matthews," he introduced himself.

"But you don't look old enough to have an eighteen-year-old daughter," she said, obviously surprised.

"Trust me, I am."

It's what happened when a guy thought with the brain south of his belt and had the first of two daughters when he was barely out of his teens.

"So you started your family when you were what? Ten?"

"Not quite." The compliment about his youthful appearance almost made him miss the fact that she hadn't yet told him who she was. This was his kitchen and he'd be the one asking the questions.

"Who are you?"

"Thea Bell."

"Why are you here?"

"Kendra didn't tell you?" Her confidence slipped and she looked uncomfortable.

What did his daughter have to do with anything? Was this woman using his child as an excuse to meet him? That wasn't ego talking. His wife had walked out on him thirteen years ago and after his divorce, he'd become fair game—fresh meat on the dating market.

At back-to-school night, there was always a divorced mom trying to get his attention. Or kids on his girls' sports teams had single mothers who invariably honed in on him. But they were barking up the wrong tree, because he had no interest in a relationship except the one he had with his daughters. After putting in a day's work at his family-owned construction company and then being both father and mother to the girls, dating didn't make the to-do list. And with Kendra just about to graduate and go on to college, he could see the light at the end of the parenting tunnel. Please, God, let it not be attached to a speeding locomotive.

He had news for Thea Bell. If her pickup approach was based on the way to a man's heart being through his stomach, she was dealing with the wrong man. He didn't care whether a woman could boil water or whip up a meal. He wasn't desperate for companionship. After his train wreck of a marriage, the single life was simple.

"What was Kendra supposed to tell me?" he asked suspiciously.

"She and I have an appointment to discuss her party."

The woman in front of him reached into the pocket of her tailored jeans and pulled out a card. He walked over to her and took it. Leaning his back against the refrigerator, he tried to ignore the sweet scent of her perfume as he read the name of her company printed in a no-nonsense font.

"For Whom the Bell Toils?" he said.

"Thea Bell toils for thee." One corner of her full mouth turned up as she shrugged. "I'm a caterer."

"Catchy." He set her card on the island in front of him and folded his arms over his chest as he studied her.

"I met Kendra at a birthday party I did for one of her friends."

"And?"

She frowned, her expression puzzled. "Did you not tell your daughter she could have a graduation party?"

"I did."

"Then why are you acting as if I'm a cat burglar who's just broken into your home to steal the fine jewelry?"

"I have no fine jewelry."

"You also didn't answer my question," she pointed out.

"I told her if she wanted a party she could be responsible for the details."

"She is being responsible for them. She's talking to a catering professional."

"When I said details, I meant buying burgers and buns at the grocery store. Not *hiring* someone to take care of the burgers and buns."

He hadn't seen her from the back, but he suspected Thea Bell had some fine buns of her own, because what he could see of her front was pretty fine. The silky white blouse tucked into her tailored jeans accentuated her breasts and a slender waist that flared into the delicate curves of her hips. He might not date much, but he still knew she was the kind of woman who would make any man instantly aware of her.

He drew in a deep breath to control the spike of his pulse. "Didn't you wonder about dealing with a teenager? Or where her parents were?"

"It's not unusual. Many parents work. They're busy and give their teenagers a lot of responsibility, especially when the teen is hosting the party. Not unlike what you said to Kendra about handling everything."

She was sharp. Using his own words against him. "How do I know you're a reputable caterer?"

"I have a list of references. You can check with the Better Business Bureau and the Santa Clarita Chamber of Commerce. If a complaint has been registered with either agency, I'll eat my spatula." She glanced at it, then back at him. "Your spatula."

It took several moments before he realized he was staring at her mouth. Her lips were plump and pink and… And giving them enough notice to attach adjectives really whipped up his irritation.

"Where is my daughter?"

"You say that as if you think I've done something with her."

"Have you?"

"Of course not," she denied. "She went up to her

room to find a picture to show me, something for the party's theme."

"Graduation isn't enough?"

"She had something in mind. For the table decorations."

"She needs decorations?"

"Technically? No." She sighed. "But it's a touch that adds an air of festivity to any gathering. It isn't just about food, it's about ambience. When guests walk in, you want them in a party mood. Decorations do that."

"And have you discussed with my daughter how much this is going to cost? And who's paying for it?"

"Not yet. I can't estimate until firm decisions are made about food, decorations and the number of guests."

"I see, so—"

Scott heard the unmistakable sound of his daughter galumphing down the stairs. A five-point-eight on the Richter scale, he estimated.

When Kendra entered the kitchen, she stopped so fast her sneakers squeaked on the tile floor. "Dad. What are you doing here?"

"I live here."

His dark-haired, blue-eyed daughter glanced from him to Thea and then back again. As much as he wished he could chalk this up to a blond moment, her hair was the wrong shade and she had guilt written all over her.

Kendra moved closer to Thea. His daughter took after him in the height department. She was tall, nearly five feet ten, and made the other woman look even smaller by comparison. "I just meant, you're home early. How come?"

"I'm meeting a real estate agent here to get a market evaluation of the house."

The teen speared him with a narrow-eyed gaze. "Define 'market evaluation,' Dad."

He should have channeled Kendra's question back to how she planned to get away with hiring a caterer when she hadn't cleared it with him. His lapse was directly due to the distraction of Thea Bell. When a man came home and found a beautiful woman in his kitchen, it tended to throw him off. Especially a man like himself, who was more comfortable with the tool belt and nail gun set. But he'd opened his mouth and now had to figure out what to do with the foot he'd inserted.

"The agent is coming to see the place and figure out how much it's worth on today's market. You know her. It's Joyce Rivers, Bernie's wife."

"I know Joyce," Thea chimed in. "We met at a Santa Clarita professional women's group. She's great."

"Why do you need Joyce to tell you how much the house is worth?" Kendra asked, refusing to be distracted.

His youngest child had been a handful since she'd turned twelve. Why should now be any different? Her older sister was an easygoing rule-follower who hadn't prepared him for Kendra's episodes of rebellion. But Kendra was going off to college soon and he wouldn't need this big house. That's why he'd arranged for Joyce to do the market evaluation and the best time for both of them happened to be when Kendra was in school. Speaking of which...

"Why aren't you in school?" he demanded.

"I told you last night," she said, sighing in exasperation as she rolled her eyes. "Today is a half-day schedule because the teachers had an end-of-quarter grading day."

"Oh. Yeah." He didn't remember her saying a word about it.

"As usual, you weren't listening." She put her hands on her hips. "You're going to sell the house, aren't you?"

Scott didn't want to have this conversation at all, let alone in front of a total stranger. "Can we talk about this later?"

"Maybe I should go," Thea said.

"Please don't," Kendra pleaded. Then she turned her patented drop-dead-you-son-of-a-bitch stare on him and huffed out a hostile breath. "Evasive tactics mean I'm right. I don't believe this. I'm not even finished with high school and you're selling my home out from under me. What if I go to the local junior college? Do you remember me telling you about that?"

"I'm not selling anything," he said, avoiding her question.

"Then why do you need to know how much the house is worth?"

"Maybe I want to refinance my loan," he countered.

"Do you?"

It was times like this when he wished he could lie. But he'd made it a point to be as honest with his daughters as he knew how. "No."

"I knew it," Kendra said. "You can't wait to get rid of me. That's why you're pushing me to go away to college."

"You're wrong, Ken. I'm not pushing you to do anything."

"You didn't want to hear about the local community college."

"I want you to have the total college experience. Like your sister—"

"Perfect Gail." The aside was directed to Thea.

"I'm sure that's not what your father meant," she said, glancing at him.

"I'm sure he did. My sister does everything right and I'm the screwup."

"Coincidentally, Joyce did a market evaluation on my condo," Thea said, changing the subject.

"Are you selling it?" Kendra asked, toning down her hostility for the caterer.

Scott almost felt sorry for Thea, getting caught in the crossfire. But his empathy was mitigated by the fact that the woman had chosen to conduct business with a teenager instead of her parent. He decided not to analyze why it seemed better to focus on Thea's error in judgment rather than her noble attempt to defuse the situation. Or his daughter's rebellious streak that had created this multi-level farce in the first place.

"Actually, I am selling," she admitted. "I'm looking for a single-family home in a nice neighborhood."

Kendra cranked the animosity back up when she looked at him. "My dad just happens to have one for sale. Maybe he'll give you a good deal. He can't wait to unload this place, along with me."

"Ken, you're being overly dramatic…"

The ringing doorbell interrupted him. If only he felt saved by the bell. "That must be Joyce now."

"I'm going to Zoe's." Kendra grabbed her purse off of the built-in desk beside the pantry and stomped out of the room.

"Kendra, wait. You know how I feel about Zoe—" When the inside door to the garage slammed, Scott sighed. Then the doorbell rang again and he went to answer it.

Thea looked around the empty kitchen feeling about as useful as one chopstick. Could this be any more awkward? She'd had dealings with teens before, but always after first contact was made by the parent and the dynamics of the working relationship were spelled out. But there was something about Kendra. When they'd met at her friend's party, she'd felt the girl reaching out. Thea had seen something in Kendra's eyes that was an awful lot like sadness. Thea figured she recognized the emotion because she'd lived with it every day for the last two years.

When Kendra had called to inquire about hiring her for a graduation party, Thea had made an exception. Today she'd brought samples of food for the teen and showed her an album of pictures displaying her work. Thea had planned to get into the business details of a signed contract and a deposit check when Scott walked in.

Kendra had only said her father was a busy building contractor who couldn't be bothered with her party. The teen hadn't mentioned how very attractive the father in question was. His dark hair, blue eyes and good looks definitely made Thea's female hormones sit up and take notice. However, her hormones had been on high alert for a while now. So her noticing him could simply be chemically induced.

But clearly his irritation about finding her in his kitchen had been all too real. Maybe if he knew how very important the party was to his daughter, he'd cut her a little slack on leaving him out of the loop.

As she stood there trying to decide what to do, Scott led Joyce Rivers into the kitchen. The tall brunette looked around. When she noticed Thea, she smiled. "Hello, there. I didn't know you and Scott knew each other."

"We just met," Thea said.

"Just," he agreed, his tone cool.

When he said nothing further, she figured he didn't

want Kendra's role in their meeting made public. But the look glittering in his very blue eyes told her his daughter would get an earful when she came home.

Joyce tapped her lip. "You know, Thea, when we talked about what you were looking for in a home, I thought about this house."

"Really?" Scott said. "Even though I hadn't decided to sell?"

"You indicated to Bernie and me that when Kendra was finished with high school, you were going to downsize. Isn't she graduating in a couple of months?"

Thea stared at him. "So Kendra's right? Her teddy bears and Barbies aren't even cold yet and you're kicking them out?"

"She's blowing things out of proportion," he said.

"Clearly she thinks you're trying to get rid of her." Thea couldn't resist making him squirm a little. Scott Matthews had walked in and treated her like a breaking and entering suspect. Maybe his daughter's issues with him weren't just the rumblings of teenage independence.

"She's wrong. It's not getting rid of her when she's going to college. What do I need with this big place?" he defended.

With one eyebrow raised, Joyce looked from Thea to Scott and back again. "Am I interrupting something?"

"No." Scott blew out a breath as he ran his fingers through his hair.

Thea folded her arms over her chest. "She was only reacting to the information that you're going to sell her childhood home out from under her."

"I'm not selling anything yet," he said. "I'm simply gathering information."

"And let's do that," Joyce said brightly. Obviously she was grateful for the excuse to change the subject. "Thea, since you're here, why don't you tag along on the tour."

"If Scott doesn't mind." She looked at him and his expression said he minded very much.

"Why not?" His enthusiasm was underwhelming.

"Great." Thea didn't care what he thought. She'd been dying to see the floor plan. Already she'd fallen in love with the kitchen. The downstairs was charming, and she was curious about the rest of the house.

She turned off the stove, then followed Joyce who was just behind Scott as he led them upstairs. Peeking around the other woman, Thea got a glimpse of his broad back narrowing to a trim waist and one fine backside. She hadn't noticed men in general, or any man in particular since she'd fallen in love with David. He'd been the love of her life and she'd lost him. Odd that the first man to make her female antenna quiver was a man who was annoyed with her.

"This is the master bedroom," he said, leading them into the room at the top of the stairs. "It goes across the back half of the house. There are his and hers walk-in closets. Double sinks and a Jacuzzi tub."

Thea fixated on the large bed because it didn't dwarf the floor space. *Not* because its owner was a big man who needed a big bed. The completely innocent thought warmed her cheeks and she forced herself to focus on his words.

"Over there, two steps down, is an area for a parent's retreat." He looked questioningly at Thea.

Was he asking if she needed a parent's retreat? Whether he was or not, she wasn't in the habit of sharing personal information, let alone her house needs, with total strangers, even above-average-looking total strangers. So the silence stretched between them.

"I haven't seen this floor plan for a long time. It's a nice room, Scott," Joyce said, filling the void. "Very large and comfortable."

Beside the master bedroom was an open loft area with a huge corner group and a big-screen TV across from it. Built-in desks were under the windows and one of them was cluttered with books and papers next to a computer. Obviously this was Kendra's work space. Her perfect older sister didn't live here any more.

Joyce looked around and took notes. "Teen rooms are popular, a good selling point."

"There's more this way," Scott said.

They peeked into the two bedrooms—one with the double bed neatly made, the other in a state of complete chaos. Obviously Kendra's. Thea didn't know why, but her heart went out to the teen who seemed to feel she didn't measure up.

Scott looked sheepish. "I had no idea her room was this bad."

"Teenagers." Joyce shrugged. "It goes with the territory."

Thea met his gaze and wondered. Shouldn't a parent have some idea about his child's environment? They lived in the same house, for goodness' sake.

"Brace yourself." He opened the bathroom door and stepped back. "I'm afraid to look."

Thea followed Joyce past him and breathed in the pleasant scent of cologne and man. Her stomach fluttered, but she chalked it up to the fact that it had been a long time since she'd experienced that particular scent. Ignoring him took some effort, but she managed to focus on the separate shower and tub area.

The vanity had two sinks and was littered with bottles of hair products and combs and brushes of various sizes and shapes. A curling iron, blow-dryer and makeup were scattered over every square inch of counter space. It seemed a million years since her biggest concern had been her hair. But she was grateful for those carefree days before she knew that life—and death—could bring her to her knees.

Sighing, she let her gaze wander. She saw flannel pajama bottoms and a coordinating top in a pile beside the overflowing wastebasket.

Scott was watching her and noticed the direction of her gaze. He hastily grabbed the handles of the trash bag, pulling it out of the container. "Sorry. I had no idea this bathroom was located in tornado alley."

Joyce arched an eyebrow. "I've seen much worse, believe me. This is nothing."

"Easy for you to say," he said, shutting the door. "I think it qualifies for federal disaster assistance."

Thea brought up the rear as they went downstairs. Was there a Mrs. Matthews? The interaction between him and his daughter gave her the impression there wasn't. The niggling sense of excitement in that thought brought her up short because it was so very unexpected.

In the kitchen, he set the bag of trash beside the tall circular metal container. "So there you have it," he said to Joyce.

She nodded. "This house will go fast on today's market."

"In spite of the biohazard bathroom?"

Thea laughed. Until his comments about Kendra's disaster of a bathroom, she'd thought the man had no sense of humor. She liked it.

"Forget it, Scott," Joyce said. "If you decide to list the place, you'll have time to clean it up."

"That will be Kendra's job," he said.

"Good luck getting her cooperation," Thea mumbled.

Joyce glanced at the two of them. "I gather she's resistant to moving?"

"She'll come around," he claimed.

"Of course she will." Joyce looked at her watch. "I've got to run to another appointment."

"So what do you think the place is worth?" he asked.

"Scott, you know as well as I do it's a gold mine. This neighborhood is one of the most desirable in Santa Clarita. Houses sell as soon as they go on the market. There's a waiting list. You can easily get top dollar."

"What kind of top dollar are we talking?"

"Let me do some comparables and I'll let you know," she said. She looked at Thea. "I'll call you about listing your condo."

Thea nodded. After Joyce was gone, she was alone with Scott Matthews. For some reason he made her nervous, and not because he was annoyed with her. It had started after her assumption that he wasn't married.

"I guess I should be going, too," she said.

"Yeah."

She looked at the food she'd brought from a luncheon and reheated here for Kendra. It didn't seem right to walk away from the dirty dishes, so she moved several pots and pans to the sink and squirted soap from the container there into them.

"Just leave that," he said.

"Can't. Part of my job. A professional doesn't leave a mess in the kitchen."

"Even though you don't have a contract?"

"Even so. It's a service-oriented, word-of-mouth business. Someone you know might need a caterer and you'll remember the one who didn't leave a mess."

While she worked, Thea glanced at Scott who brooded beside her. "Kendra told me she's never had a party. Is that true?"

He met her gaze and his own narrowed. "It doesn't mean she's underprivileged."

"I can see that she's got everything she needs. Materially," she added.

"What are you saying?"

"Just that I got the feeling it was very important to her to have a party."

"What was your first clue, Dr. Phil?"

She ignored his sarcasm. "The fact that she didn't tell you I was coming. I'd have to guess she felt you would veto the catering idea."

"She didn't give me a chance to veto it."

"And if she had? What would you have said?" Thea asked, watching him carefully.

He sighed. "Probably I'd have said no."

"Look…" She rested her wrists inside the sink, letting the water drip from her hands. "Probably I should have asked if she had permission to hire me. And when it came to a signed contract and deposit check, the cat would have been out of the bag. But there's something about Kendra."

"Why didn't she come to me? That's a rhetorical question by the way." He shook his head, then met her gaze. "And I don't understand why she's so upset about selling the house. It's just a house." His tone oozed frustration.

"Men." Thea stared at him, not bothering to conceal her exasperation.

"What?"

His clueless express was so darn cute, she couldn't help a small sigh. "How long have you lived here?"

He thought for a moment and said, "I guess ten or eleven years."

"So Kendra was about seven or eight when you moved in. She hardly remembers living anywhere else. She's facing big changes, like leaving high school and going away to college. Then she finds out you're getting rid of her anchor. Of course she freaked. Change is hard."

"I haven't gotten rid of anything yet."

"Just the thought of change is uncomfortable. It's human nature to fight against that."

Scott shifted his feet and brushed against the bag of trash on the floor. It tilted sideways, spilling the contents. "Damn it."

He bent to pick up the bag, giving her an unobstructed view of his backside. She was the first to admit she was out of practice in the fine art of observing men. And truthfully, she'd never understood the fascination for that particular part of the male anatomy. But Scott Matthews' fanny gave her a completely different perspective.

He straightened, pressed the latch on the kitchen can and dumped the smaller bag inside. Then he stooped again to gather up the stray trash on the tile. He picked up a slender plastic stick.

Frowning, he rolled it between his fingers. "Is this what I think it is?"

She saw the plus and minus symbols. "It is if you think it's a pregnancy test."

She should know. She'd used one not that long ago and hers had come up a plus.

Chapter Two

"Just shoot me now." A muscle jumped in Scott's lean cheek and tension made his already square jaw seem harder somehow. "Does this mean it's negative?"

Thea stared at the minus sign. "Not necessarily. The results are only accurate for a short time. There's no way to know if it's positive or negative unless you know how long it's been lying around."

His expression was dark when he looked up. "I feel as if I've been walking down the stairs and just missed the last three steps."

She wiped her hands on a dish towel. "Don't jump to conclusions."

Impossibly blue eyes narrowed on her. "What are you? Twenty-seven? Twenty-eight?"

"Thirty-four." But what did that have to do with anything?

"Married? Divorced?"

"Neither," she answered. "I'm a widow."

Something flickered in his eyes, but she was grateful when he didn't comment. The automatic "I'm sorry" was awkward and meaningless. She wasn't even sure why she'd clarified her marital status to him. Normally she didn't volunteer anything like that. But nothing about today was normal.

"Do you have any children?" he asked, exasperation lacing his tone.

Not yet, although she would soon. God willing. But this man was grilling her like raw hamburger. She'd innocently gotten caught up in his personal problems; that didn't mean she had to reciprocate with her own problems. When her husband had received his cancer diagnosis, she'd learned the very hard lesson that personal information should be dispensed on a need-to-know basis. Scott was a prospective client. Maybe not, she thought, noting his intense expression. But whatever happened, he wasn't entitled to her life story.

And she certainly wasn't going to tell this man, this virtual stranger, that she was now pregnant through in vitro fertilization with her dead husband's baby. She couldn't ignore the question, but there was no need to put a finer point on it.

"No," she finally said. "I don't have any children."

He slid her an I-thought-so look. "Then don't tell me not to jump to conclusions."

"I was simply trying to help."

"There's nothing you can do. This," he said, holding up the stick, "means she's having sex. Probably unprotected."

"I'm not an idiot, Scott. I know this is a serious issue."

"Really?" He put the test stick on the counter beside him, then met her gaze. "You know it intellectually? Or because you've watched Oprah and Dr. Phil? Or you've seen the teenage pregnancy statistics in *Newsweek?*"

"Of course, but—"

"But you don't have children. You have no idea what it's like to be nineteen and find out you're going to be a father. You don't have a clue what it's like to be a kid yourself and find out you're going to have a baby."

"No, but—"

"I do," he interrupted. "It's damned scary. And everyone has an opinion about what should happen. My parents. Her parents. On top of that, she and I couldn't agree on what to do."

"What *did* you do?" Thea couldn't stop herself from asking. Just because she had a hang-up about sharing nonessential personal information didn't mean she wasn't curious about him. If he had a problem with it, he could tell her to mind her own business.

"I married her," he answered.

"Most people would call that doing the right thing."

"The right thing?" His handsome features turned harsh.

"No one could call your daughter ugly names or tease her about being born outside of marriage."

"Yeah, at least I prevented that." He smiled, but there was no humor in the look.

"And it can't have been all bad. You had a second child together."

He folded his arms over his chest. "Kendra wasn't planned. We were still too young and, I thought, perfectly happy with one child. Then we were careless. I was all of twenty-two when she came along."

Thea thought about her own struggle to become a mother. Ever since she was a little girl, she'd wanted to have a baby. When she'd married, she'd ached to know what it was like to feel a life growing inside her. She felt it now, mostly because she was tired and nauseous. The point was, she felt *different,* important. After the heartbreak of two miscarriages, she yearned to bring a healthy baby into the world and would do everything possible to make that happen. Now Scott was telling her his second child wasn't welcome.

She didn't try to hide the irritation and disapproval she suspected were visible on her face. "Some people would say having two children makes you lucky."

"I am. And very grateful they're normal, healthy kids. I love them more than anything. But the fact is I missed out on a lot. I hardly got to be a kid before I had two in two and a half years."

"But isn't it the tough times that forge the bonds in a relationship?"

"Not ours. That second pregnancy was the straw that broke the camel's back."

"What do you mean?"

"When Gail was seven and Kendra five, she decided the girls and I were cramping her style. She didn't want to be a mother and she left."

"She abandoned her children?"

"Define abandoned. Every once in a while she turns up. It was worse when they were little and all their emotions were stirred up. Now the girls have her pegged. They're polite but cool if she drops in."

"It must have hurt them a lot."

"They're better off without her." He shrugged. "They got over it."

Did they? And were they really better off without her? Thea wondered. Through no fault of their own or Scott's, Kendra and her sister hadn't been raised by Ward and June Cleaver. And Thea sensed ripples beneath the surface in the Matthews household. Sensed, heck. She'd seen for herself the tension between Scott and his daughter. Kendra was still hurting.

"Were you better off when your wife left?" she asked him. Again she wondered if he would answer. In his shoes, she wouldn't. But everything she'd just learned had her curiosity sparring with her better judgment.

He sighed. "That's not an easy question to answer. It was tough doing it alone. I still had to work to put food on the table and a roof over our heads. But I had two little girls depending on me when they got sick. Child care was a constant worry. And it's expensive. There was no one to share the responsibility."

That gave Thea a pang. Her plan of having a baby had always included sharing the experience with her baby's father. And the plan had always involved sex with said father. She'd never envisioned that the love of her life would get sick. That he would simply donate sperm and medical science would take care of the rest. She was having a baby. And she would be doing it alone. But in her case, she would never know what having help and support felt like, so she wouldn't feel the absence of it. But Scott *had* known.

"Did you miss her? Or was it just parenting alone that was a problem? I'm sorry," she said, before he could answer. She held up her hand. "That's really none of my business."

What was it about Scott Matthews that made inappropriate questions pop out of her mouth?

"Actually, the fact that I don't mind you asked is an answer in itself. Yes, I missed her. And not just because raising those two girls alone was the hardest thing I've ever done in my life."

He'd cared and then he was alone. She related all too well. "I'm sorry," she said again.

"I don't need sympathy. Raising kids is also the most wonderful, rewarding thing I've ever done." He blew out a long breath. "I'm not exactly sure why I told you all that."

"Maybe because I happened to be here when you found the stick?"

He frowned. "That damn pregnancy test."

"Sometimes it's easier to confide in strangers. Someone who doesn't have an emotional stake in any of this."

"Yeah," he said, running his fingers through his hair. "I don't usually spill my guts. But then, it's not every day I find out my daughter is sexually active."

"Shock will loosen your tongue."

He glanced at the evidence beside him. "I can't believe this. I don't want my daughter to be a mother while she's still a child herself. I don't want her to repeat my mistakes."

"I hate to think of children as mistakes," she said, a tad sharply. "They're a consequence of an action. A fact of life." Or in her case, combining her egg with her husband's sperm in a petri dish. In vitro fertilization was the miracle that had produced her fact of life.

"You're splitting hairs. I don't want them to do the same things I did. And now I find this."

"You were right when you said I've had no experience in this area. But you're obviously upset and I feel compelled to offer something. If Kendra is pregnant, it would be an experience that will take her down a different path. It doesn't have to mean failure for either of you."

"Hold on—"

"Think about it," she interrupted. "Can you honestly tell me you can imagine your life without your children in it?"

Hostility crackled in the air between them. Then the corners of his mouth curved up. "Actually, yes. I've been imagining Kendra going off to college."

"She'll still be in your life," Thea pointed out.

"I was kidding. She thinks I'm against junior college. Truthfully, I have mixed feelings about her going away. You're right. I can't imagine never having my girls. They're my reason for getting out of bed every day and putting one foot in front of the other."

Boy, in her current condition, she could really relate to that. It was on the tip of her tongue to tell him about her pregnancy, to share it with him. To bond. But she swallowed the temptation.

"Look, Scott, has it occurred to you that the test might not even belong to her?"

His face brightened. "Actually, no."

"You're obviously a glass-is-half-empty kind of guy," she said wryly. "It's always possible that it belongs to a friend who didn't want to take the test at her house. And Kendra was just being supportive."

"Way to put a positive spin on this."

His sudden smile had a very weird effect on her. She felt the force of it through her whole body. Her stomach dropped as if she were riding an elevator that suddenly plunged toward the basement. And her heart fluttered as if powered by a horde of humming birds' wings.

"I'm a pro at spinning," she finally managed to say.

"Spinning the facts?"

"No, actually. Salad spinning is more my style."

"Thanks for the benefit of an alternate perspective."

He laughed. "But seriously, I'm sorry I dumped on you."

"Like I could have stopped you." She smiled.

"You could have left."

"No, I really couldn't. I've never met anyone who looked like they needed to talk more than you did today. And it is helpful, especially if somebody listens."

"I don't normally get carried away like that."

"No problem. Don't give it another thought."

Thea sincerely meant that. She had a feeling Scott's daughter was searching for an emotional *something*. And the pregnancy test was troubling. She was aware that the girl had reached out to her, even if it was behind her father's back. Obviously her graduation party was a big deal to Kendra and for some reason she couldn't tell her father.

"But do me a favor, Scott."

"Sure. What?"

"Just keep in mind that some girls confuse—"

The garage door slammed just before Kendra walked into the family room. She looked at the two of them. "Hi, Thea."

Scott felt the hostility radiating from his daughter. Even if he hadn't, he wasn't ready for the conversation he knew he had to have with her. "How is Zoe?"

"She wasn't home." She glared at him. "How come you're still here?"

Talking to Thea had begun to calm him down, but he could feel his blood pressure climbing again. He glanced at Thea and saw the sympathy on her face as she quietly watched Kendra.

"What does that mean?" he asked.

Kendra lifted one shoulder. The sullen gesture was one he saw from time to time and it never failed to fire up his frustration. "You're selling the house," she said. "Your work here is done. I figured you'd go back to the office."

He picked up the pregnancy test stick and held it up. "Not after I found this."

Kendra's eyes grew wide. Then surprise was replaced with angry resentment. "You were snooping in my stuff?"

"If you call dumping the trash in your bathroom snooping—yes."

Thea picked up her purse. "Scott. Kendra. You two need to talk. It would probably be best if I leave you alone."

"Don't go," Kendra said. "I want you to stay."

"But, this is private." Thea took a step back.

"Not anymore. Thanks to my Dad."

"Don't make this about me," he defended. "If you straightened up after yourself, I'd never have known. Your room—"

"You were in my room?" Her voice rose in pitch to just below what only a dog could hear.

"Yes. And you know why."

"To sell it." Kendra huffed out a breath.

"It's part of the house."

"I can't believe you let strangers in my room."

Thea cleared her throat and slid her purse on her shoulder. "I'll just get my things together."

"Please don't go," Kendra begged. "I didn't mean you're a stranger."

But she was. Practically. Scott looked between the two of them. "Why is it so important for her to stay?"

"Neutral third party," his daughter said, tossing a strand of hair over her shoulder. "I need a witness."

Scott looked at his daughter, the dark hair and blue eyes that were so like his. Maybe that's what scared him

the most—that she was so much like him. A little rebellious. A little daring. Hostile and angry. The thought
of her making the same mistakes and living with the
consequences tied him in knots. He wanted her to have
more choices, fewer problems. Hell, he wanted her life
to be perfect, however unrealistic that was. How did he
get through to her?

He looked at Thea, who was studying him. If it
would help Kendra, he had no objection to Thea stick-
ing around. After spilling his guts, there wasn't a whole
lot she didn't know. He nodded slightly and she took
her purse off her shoulder.

"Now, forget about the house," he said, glancing at
the pregnancy test. "There's something more important
we have to focus on."

"That's none of your business."

"I disagree," he shot back. "I'm your father. If you're
having sex—"

"I don't want to talk to you about this."

"I don't care. Are you pregnant?" he demanded.

"That's none of your business," she said angrily.

"The hell it's not. You're my daughter."

"An accident of birth doesn't give you the right to
tell me what to do."

"Actually it does. And another reason I can is that I
pay all the bills around here."

"There won't be an 'around here' much longer,
thanks to you," she said.

He glanced at Thea, who was diplomatically silent.
Then he met his daughter's angry gaze. "It's not going
to work."

"What?" she asked defiantly.

"You're trying to take the heat off by changing the
subject."

"And you don't give a damn about my feelings."

"If you're talking about the house again, I'm not going there." He took a step forward. "Focus, Kendra. That pregnancy test tells me you're having sex. I need to know if you're going to have a baby and who the father is."

Like heat rising from blacktop, animosity rolled off the teen in waves. "I can't believe you. For the last eighteen years, you've practically ignored me. I'm eighteen. I'm an adult, too old for you to interfere in my life."

"You'll never be too old. And I'll always be your father. It's my job to interfere."

"Why can't you just leave this alone? Leave me alone?"

Scott felt frustration and anger coiling inside him, but struggled to control the feelings. Before he could, she turned and ran from the room. "Kendra? Come back here," he shouted.

The stomping on the stairs was a good indication that she planned to ignore him. He started to go after her.

"Scott?"

He felt a hand on his arm and looked at Thea. "What?"

"It might be best to let her go."

"But I have to know."

Thea's brown eyes were warm with sympathy. "And she'll just continue to stonewall you if you charge after her."

"So? I'll wear her down."

Thea shook her head. "Not in her present state of mind, you won't. You can talk, but you can't force her to reveal anything."

When she removed her hand from his arm, he missed the warmth of her fingers. "Do you have a suggestion?"

"Yes."

"Care to share?"

She nodded. "Give her some space. Let her calm down. You might want to do the same."

"I am calm."

"Oh?" Thea blinked up at him and then she smiled.

"What's so funny?" he asked.

"You're stretched so tight, if you were a rubber band and let go, you'd put someone's eye out."

He released a long breath. "Okay. Maybe you're right." He stared at the doorway where his daughter had stood moments before. "But I don't get it. What was all that about ignoring her for eighteen years?"

"I don't know," Thea said.

"Maybe this is payback."

"For what? Being a good father?"

He looked at her. "For how I felt when I first found out my wife was pregnant again. But when I saw Kendra for the first time…" He searched for words to express the power of his emotions and couldn't find any. "It was love at first sight," he finally said.

"Have you ever told *her* that?"

"I don't know." He rubbed the back of his neck.

"Under the circumstances, she might have some unresolved feelings," Thea suggested. "Some girls confuse sex and love."

"Are you saying she's looking for love in all the wrong places because she thinks I don't care about her?"

"I have no idea." She sighed. "I'm just the caterer. They say the way to a man's heart is through his stomach. I'm not sure there's a parallel, but she contacted me to do her graduation party. And she didn't tell you she was doing the party on that scale. I'm no shrink, but it's obvious to me that she's sending you some kind of message."

"Can you decode it?"

"With my magic garlic press? Or maybe the decoder in my secret slotted spoon?" she asked, one corner of her full mouth tilting up.

"Okay. Stupid question. But you're a woman. Do you have any thoughts about what she's trying to say?"

"Yes."

When she didn't say anything further he added, "Any you'd care to share?"

"Do you really want me to? After all, I've never had any children," she said pointedly.

"Okay. I deserve that for patronizing you. But I'm desperate. Lady, I need all the help I can get. If you've got any ideas, I'm listening."

"Okay." She nodded. "I suggest you give her some time. When she's ready to talk, you listen to her."

"That's it?"

She nodded, then said, "And one more thing."

"Yes?"

"Think about having the party, and not just an average backyard barbecue. Give some thought to doing it the way she wants it," she added.

"Because you need the gig?"

She shook her head. "I don't need the job badly enough to take advantage of your situation. If one job was that important, I wouldn't be looking to take on a bigger house and mortgage."

"Okay. Then why should I think about doing the shindig her way?"

"Because my impression is that she's basically a good kid. And this was important enough to her to go behind your back."

"So you're saying I should reward her bad behavior?"

She thought for a moment and then said, "Think of it as hearing her cry for help. If she knows you're listening instead of lecturing, she's more likely to tell you what you want to know."

"How can I just listen when I need to make her understand that if she's not careful, she could ruin her life?"

"If I could answer that question, I'd be a financially independent woman." Thea shrugged and smiled a little sadly. "Goodbye, Scott. Good luck," she added.

It was odd, but when he'd found her in his kitchen, he'd been irritated. Watching her leave irritated him even more. And the implications of that didn't sweeten his temper.

Chapter Three

The following morning Thea parked her car in front of her office, then went to let herself in. She found the door was unlocked, which meant her workaholic partner was already there.

"Connie?" she called out, setting her purse and briefcase on her desk.

"Back here," came the reply.

She'd been best friends with Connie Howard since the seventh grade. They'd gone through everything together—their weddings, the birth of her friend's two children and the death of Thea's husband. She would have gotten through it without Connie, but probably not with her sanity intact.

Thea walked through the doorway separating the front office from the kitchen/work area in the back. She'd leased this space when her business outgrew her condo. Sometimes she cooked for a job at home, but mostly she and Connie prepared food here.

They'd furnished this office with a top-of-the-line double oven, a microwave/convection oven, a large side-by-side refrigerator and the best set of pots and pans their budget allowed. The drawers and cupboards were stuffed with the latest gizmos to make a cook's heart go pitter-patter.

Connie was industriously wiping down the countertops. As Thea approached, her tall, redheaded friend glanced over her shoulder. "Hi, T."

"Hi, yourself. It's only eight-thirty. What are you doing here so early?"

"It's not *that* early. Besides, I had a day off." She faced Thea and put her hands on her boyishly slim hips. "So how did your appointments go yesterday?"

The image of Scott Matthews instantly popped into her head. Not surprising, since thoughts of him hadn't been far from her mind since leaving his place yesterday. She'd wondered whether his daughter was going to have a baby. Some appointment.

"I took deposits for several parties," she said vaguely.

Connie's green-eyed gaze narrowed on her. "And?"

"And nothing."

"Don't blow me off, T. You've got a funny look on your face."

Thea sat on one of the tall stools outside the U-shaped work space and looked at her friend. "One of my appointments got a little weird. The initial contact was made by a teenager who didn't have parental permission for a catered graduation party."

"Bummer."

"Yeah," Thea said, sighing with what felt like regret. And she wasn't sure why. Like she'd told Scott—it wasn't as if they needed the catering job to survive. This business was thriving and word of mouth was their best free advertising.

Connie leaned forward and rested her elbows on the counter. "It's just as well you found out she was pulling a fast one before putting time, effort and money into the event. How did the underhanded little stinker get caught?"

"Kendra's father came home unexpectedly while she and I were discussing the party."

"What about the kid's mother?"

"Out of the picture," Thea answered. "And I get the feeling Kendra is having some feelings about it. She accused her father of ignoring her."

"I was going to high-five you on your perception, but most teenagers are giddy with happiness when their parents ignore them. I'd say that's a big clue she's got issues."

Thea laughed. "There's more."

"How can there be more? Is this kid in training for *America's Most Wanted?* How old is she?"

"She's eighteen, getting ready to graduate and go to college. Scott wants—"

"Scott?"

"Her father. He wants her to go away to school and she was talking up the local junior college. Reading between the lines, I think maybe she's getting cold feet."

"So she's acting out? Masterminding a covert event to get even with a pushy dad?"

Thea shook her head. "Your flair for the dramatic comes in handy for planning themed events. But in everyday life, not so much."

"I'm not the one trying to pull a fast one," Connie protested.

"Maybe she has reason. She was upset about her father getting ready to sell the house when she goes to college. He hadn't said anything to her about it yet. Selling, I mean."

"Still, he's the grown-up. I don't think a failure to communicate is cause to take him out back and beat the crap out of him. So to speak," she added.

Thea shrugged. "I think he's guilty of premeditated failure to communicate. He didn't want to deal with his daughter's emotional fallout until it was absolutely necessary."

"Chicken," Connie said.

"I can't say I blame him."

"Now you're defending him?" her friend questioned.

"I guess it's my tragic flaw that I can see both sides of an issue. He was somewhat hostile in the beginning. But then I began to feel sorry for him."

"Why?"

Thea rested her chin on her knuckles. "I guess it was the pregnancy test he found."

"Whoa." Connie shook her head as if to clear it. "You're going to need to back up and explain that one."

"It's not that complicated. Joyce took a tour of the house for the market evaluation and I tagged along. It's a great place, by the way. Just what I've been looking for."

"Yeah, yeah. Get back to the test."

"Kendra's bathroom looked like a beauty supply store threw up all over it. He was shocked and appalled in equal parts and instinctively grabbed the bag of trash. When he was dumping it, the little stick fell out."

"Is she pregnant?"

Thea lifted one shoulder in a shrug. "Inconclusive because it's only accurate for a certain length of time. He didn't know how long ago she'd done the test before tossing it in the trash."

"Did you tell him you knew this because you'd recently used one yourself?"

Thea shook her head. "He was in a state of shock and didn't ask how I could read it."

"And if he had?"

"I'd have told him it's none of his business. My pregnancy has barely gotten off the ground. In my experience, it's bad luck bordering on a jinx to talk about it until I've successfully completed the first trimester."

"Okay."

The tone of that one word said she was crazy and superstitious.

"Connie, don't you go judgmental on me. You know better than anyone why I feel this way. In vitro fertilization is personal and private. I've done it twice and twice I thought I was pregnant. The first time, I told everyone. Strangers on the street, people on the phone, it didn't matter. And then I lost the baby. I had to go back to everyone I'd told and relive the pain of losing a child over and over. But once wasn't enough. I did it again because apparently I'm incapable of learning from my mistake. Third time's the charm. I won't do it again. Especially because I've got all my eggs in one basket. So to speak. I have no more eggs, at least none that are fertilized."

"I'm aware of that. And, by the way, that was quite a speech."

"It's from the heart, Con. If I lose this baby, too, it will be like losing my husband all over again." She took a deep breath to relieve the sudden pressure in her chest. "I promised David I would make sure part of him went on."

"And you've done that," Connie said, sympathy lacing the words.

"Not yet. Not until this child is born. To do that, I will not breathe a word to anyone—"

"What am I? Chopped liver?"

"You're my best friend. I had to tell you. Besides, you'd have known. Sort of a best friend ESP." She shrugged. "But I will not discuss this baby with anyone else until the first trimester is under my belt."

"So to speak."

"Yes." Thea reluctantly gave in to a smile.

"Not even your family?"

"Especially not them. Mom and Dad can't be emotionally involved until the risky first three months are done. They were crushed the other two times and I don't want them hurt again. Or my brother and sister, either."

"You don't need to protect everyone, Thea."

"Not everyone. Just my family, including this life inside me. Con, I can't remember a time when I didn't want children. Even when I was a little girl, I was drawn to babies. When I see a pregnant woman, or someone with kids in a stroller, the yearning to have one is so powerful, it's almost a pain inside me. Does that sound crazy?"

"Yes." Connie tucked a strand of red hair behind her ear. "But I understand. If I'd never had a couple of little misery-makers, I know I'd feel as if something was missing from my life."

Connie's choice of words belied the fact that she was a devoted wife and mother. She'd been Thea's rock through everything: when Thea and David were trying unsuccessfully to conceive; the subsequent exams that indirectly led to discovering his cancer; freezing sperm so they could have children following his chemotherapy; remission; the two IVF attempts that were unsuccessful and so incredibly heartbreaking; David's relapse and death. Now this one last try.

"I will do anything," Thea said, "to insure the success of this pregnancy."

"And I'll help in any way I can." Connie made a gesture, as if she were zipping her lips.

"Thanks."

Connie grinned. "So tell me about Scott Matthews."

"He's got baggage, big-time."

"Who doesn't?"

"You, for one." Thea toyed with the diamond-studded heart on a delicate chain around her neck. "He's raised his two girls on his own—a father for the first time at twenty. It was an enormous responsibility and he was understandably upset to learn his daughter used a pregnancy test. And concerned she'll repeat his history."

"Wow, that's a lot of information."

"I guess he felt comfortable talking to me. That happens sometimes with a complete stranger."

"And how would you know that? Sharing information isn't something you do," Connie pointed out.

"And you know why. When David was sick, I found out the hard way that sharing details can be a huge mistake." One she didn't plan to repeat. Burn me once, shame on you. Burn me twice, shame on me.

"Still," Connie said, "there's something different about you since I last saw you."

"Probably the pregnancy glow," she said wryly. "Although I think that's an old wives' tale. I haven't got the energy to glow."

"Don't be so sure. There's a sparkle in your eyes. Could it be because of Scott Matthews?"

"I think someone's been whacked with the whimsical stick," Thea said. "I'm the same as usual. Besides, Scott joked about wanting to be alone when his daughter goes to college. But I think many a truth is spoken in jest."

Thea could tell him, alone wasn't all it's cracked up to be. She wouldn't share that with her friend and give her any ideas. But the truth was, as a caterer, she cooked for many people, but no one special. There was no one waiting for her at home, no one to take care of, no one to talk about her day with.

"No one's whacked me with anything," Connie said. "I just know you. What does Scott Matthews look like?"

"Oh, come on—"

"Humor me."

Thea let out a big sigh. "He's tall. Dark hair. Blue eyes."

"Not bad. What does he do for a living?"

"Kendra told me he's a building contractor," Thea answered. "And if his house is any indication, he does all right financially."

"So you had this communication thing going on, yet you're blowing him off?"

"He was annoyed that I met with his daughter behind his back. For Whom the Bell Toils didn't get the job. I have no reason to see him again. That doesn't constitute blowing him off. There's nothing to blow off."

She heard the ding-dong from the reception area indicating someone had come in the front door. "Anyone here?" The voice was decidedly masculine.

"I'll get it," Connie said, untying her apron.

"No. I'll go. Saved by the bell." Thea stood and grinned at her friend. "Now I know how Kendra felt when her father started in on her."

Thea walked through the door and was surprised to see the father in question standing there. Her stomach did a funny little shimmy. She knew it was too early for that movement to be about the baby. So it had to be all about Scott Matthews. She hadn't expected to be attracted to a man again. She'd thought that part of her had died with her husband.

She smiled at Scott. "Hello again."

"Thea." One corner of his wonderful mouth quirked up. "Or should I call you Obi-Wan?"

"Excuse me?"

"You did see *Star Wars?*"

"Of course. But I don't get the reference."

"The teacher and the student. Are you sure you don't have children?"

None that she'd cop to just yet. "No. I mean yes, I'm sure. Why? What are you talking about?"

"Wise you are, as well as beautiful," he said, imitating one of the movie characters.

"I think that's Yoda-speak. But if it was a bona fide compliment, thank you."

"It was. And you're welcome."

"Why am I wise?" she asked, refusing to acknowledge the beautiful part of that compliment.

"I managed to talk to Kendra without anyone leaving the room in hysterics, including me."

She laughed. "What happened?"

"I took your advice and simply listened and asked questions. I tried not to lecture or offer advice."

"And that didn't make you hysterical?" she couldn't resist asking.

"Of course it did. I'm a guy. And I build things. So the need to fix it *now* is especially strong. But I was a brave little soldier and didn't let it show."

"Wow. Congressional Medal of Honor material."

He leaned a jean-clad hip against her desk and half

sat. "It almost killed me not to bring up the pregnancy test, but I tried it your way."

"And?"

"She admitted she feels bad when there's an event and her mother isn't there. Which proves your theory— listen you must, then talk to you she will."

Thea laughed. "I didn't say it like that."

"No. But the message was the same. I hope by not lecturing this time, she'll be more open to talking about it when I bring up the subject of the pregnancy test. Which I plan to in the very near future." He frowned and worry lines bracketed his nose and mouth.

"Good instincts. Pick and choose your battles. Figure out which hill you want to die on."

"Actually, I'd prefer not to die on any of them. But I suppose a single battle isn't critical as long as I win the war."

"Well said, General Solo." She saluted. His responding grin hit her in the midsection like a fireball. She backed away and rested her backside against Connie's desk.

"I—I'm glad you think I helped," she said, hoping he hadn't noticed her stammer. And especially hoping he didn't get that her reaction to him caused it. "But, really, I didn't do anything. There should be some kind of a medal for raising a terrific young woman like Kendra. I'm sure your older daughter is just as wonderful."

"Gail," he said.

She nodded. "She's in college and on her way, thanks to you."

"I don't know how much is thanks to me. She's just a good kid. So is Kendra." He ran his fingers through his hair. "I always thought I was doing a good job as both mother and father. That they wouldn't miss their mother too much. After listening to my daughter, I realize I was wrong. She missed a lot."

"It's not your fault, Scott. You shouldn't feel guilty."

"No? I picked the woman who walked out so who else is there to blame?"

"You couldn't make her stay. Any more than—"

"What?" he prompted.

She'd been about to say any more than she could prevent her husband from dying. But this conversation wasn't about her. It was about a breakthrough with his daughter. Thea knew saying something about her own loss would completely shift the topic to her. Talking about herself could get awkward.

"I was going to say you couldn't make her stay any more than you could keep your girls from growing up."

"Isn't that the truth?" A tender look stole into his eyes. "But I wanted to give my kids everything, every advantage. And I couldn't give them a mom, which is what they needed most."

The words were like a stone pressing on Thea's chest. She'd made a choice to do everything humanly possible to ensure that a part of her husband went on. Now she was well on her way to keeping her promise. But she'd never stopped to consider the child's feelings. Scott's ex-wife was alive and well somewhere and, if she had a change of heart, could be involved with her girls. But there was no way her child would ever know its father.

How profoundly sad was that? When she and David had first started trying to have a baby, she'd had dreams about parenting together. She so very much wanted to share the experience with him. But fate had other plans. Now she was in this alone. And Scott was alone, too.

For a long time now. Why was that? A good-looking guy like him. Was he commitment-phobic? If so, she certainly couldn't blame him.

"Thea?"

"Hmm?" She looked up and noticed Scott was frowning.

"You drifted off there. Anything wrong?"

"No." She took a deep breath. "I was just wondering—"

"What?"

"Feel free to tell me to jump in the lake. But I was wondering how a mother could simply walk out on her children."

"There's the million-dollar question." He lifted one broad shoulder drawing her attention there.

His light blue collared golf shirt molded to his upper body in a most intriguing way. He was alternately lean and muscular in all the right places. Her gaze slid to the sturdy work boots he wore and she tried to remember if she'd always thought the look was sexy. Or if it was more a matter of the man *in* the boots.

He sighed. "I was focused on how hard her leaving was on me and the difficulties of raising the girls alone. They seemed to be doing fine, so I took that at face value. I believed it because it was easier. I buried my head in the sand and left my backside exposed."

And a very nice backside it was, Thea thought. Unfortunately, she'd noticed a lot more than his backside and had the spiking pulse and sweaty palms to prove it.

"You've obviously done a fine job with the girls, Scott. And that's the last time I'm going to pump up your ego. It's entirely possible that Kendra hasn't missed her mother all that much. Until now. Graduation from high school is a big step. I still remember the emotional trauma."

"Really?" He folded his arms over his chest. The movement showcased his superior biceps.

"Spoken like a man," she said, shaking her head. "She's grieving the loss of a comfortable way of life as well as the familiar faces she sees every day."

"But she'll make new friends in college."

"She doesn't know that yet. All she can see is what will be gone. What's changing. Maybe this has triggered some emotional upheaval she hasn't felt until now."

He rubbed the back of his neck. "Interesting theory. She's had bouts of rebelliousness here and there. But until yesterday, she's never done anything without running it by me first."

"Reading between the lines, I'd say that behavior is an indication of something pretty important to her."

"Yeah. When I listened to her, I got that impression."

Thea knew men were action-oriented, and Scott more than most. She wondered how many fathers would have taken her advice and actually listened to their daughters. She met his gaze across the space separating the desks and realized he was certainly more than just another pretty face. In addition to his good looks, he was thoughtful, introspective and boyishly charming. The triple threat.

She had a vague sense of relief that she hadn't gotten the catering job. He was the first man she'd noticed in a long time and the sensation wasn't the least bit comfortable. She didn't want to notice a man. It was act one in a play she wouldn't audition for.

Obviously Scott had dropped by to thank her for the advice. And the courtesy was very nice. But she was grateful she wouldn't have to see him again after this.

"I appreciate the 4-1-1 about Kendra."

"Hmm?" he said, obviously puzzled.

"Information. That she's communicating," Thea clarified.

"Yeah." He blew out a long breath.

She straightened away from the desk. "I'm glad things went well with the two of you. Now I have to get to an appointment."

He stood up. "And I have to get to work."

"Kendra said you're a building contractor?"

"Matthews and Sons Construction. My father is retired now, but my brother and I run the company."

"Aren't you doing that big housing project over in Northbridge?"

He nodded. "And I have a crew there waiting for me."

"You shouldn't keep them waiting any longer. Thanks for stopping by, Scott."

"Actually, I didn't come by just to give you an update. I want to hire Thea Bell to toil for me. Will you cater my daughter's graduation party?"

Talk about burying your head in the sand. Thea hadn't seen that one coming. Or maybe she just hadn't wanted to see it. Now what was she going to do?

Chapter Four

"You want to hire me?"

"That's what I said. You sound surprised."

"That's because I am." There was an understatement, she thought.

"Why?"

"I guess because you acted as if I committed a mortal sin when I treated your daughter like a grown-up."

"I may have overreacted," he admitted. "I might have come off a tad abrasive."

She couldn't resist needling him *a tad*. "Might have? You acted as if I was working black-ops catering with your teenager behind your back. I got the impression that my integrity was questionable in your opinion."

"Now that you mention it…" His expression turned sheepish. "I made some phone calls. You'll be glad to know your integrity checks out fine."

"What a relief. I was worried."

When he turned all the amps in his grin on her, Thea

couldn't breathe. She began to straighten the already neat stack of receipts on Connie's desk, but the distraction didn't do much to take the edge off her reaction to him. He was offering her a job. The fact that she was even hesitating to take it spoke volumes. When she was dealing with Kendra, there had been no question about her doing the party. Now that she would be dealing with Kendra's father, everything was different. And it shouldn't be.

Thea had catered events for both women and men. She'd done functions for corporate CEOs—*male* executives. This man was no different.

And that was when she recognized the lie.

She liked Scott and that made him different. It made her as nervous as a dieter in a doughnut shop, which was why she wanted to turn him down flat.

Then she looked head-on into the intensity of his gaze and her stomach did that whole stop, drop and roll thing. From another lifetime she vaguely remembered this feeling. It was another good reason to refuse the job. But what did that intensity in his expression mean? Did he find her attractive? It had been too long since she'd wondered or cared about such things and she couldn't tell. Her feminine instincts, too long turned off, were now unreliable. He probably didn't care about her one way or the other and she was being a ninny.

"Earth to Thea. It didn't take this long to build the Suez Canal. So what do you say? Will you take the gig?"

"Do you have a date in mind?" she hedged. "I need to check my schedule."

"She's graduating the middle of June, assuming there are no unexpected surprises with her grades. But she's always been an honors student, so I don't expect that." He thought for a moment. "I think a Saturday night would work best." Moving closer to her, he glanced down at the large, desk-blotter calendar. "How about June nineteenth?" he said, pointing to the date.

She noticed the strength in his wide wrist and tanned forearm. She watched the muscles there bunch and ripple, making it difficult for her to take a deep breath.

"I'll check my day planner." She unzipped her briefcase and pulled out the leather-bound calendar. After opening it, she found the date and tried not to let him see her relief when she spotted a conflict. Loophole. She met his gaze. "I'm holding that date open for someone."

"Holding it?" He frowned. "I'm going to take a shot in the dark here. Do you have a signed contract? A deposit?"

"Not yet, but I promised to try and keep that date free and I feel an obligation to the client."

He pulled a checkbook from the back pocket of his jeans. "I'm willing to sign on the dotted line right now and put my money where my mouth is."

Of course as soon as he mentioned it, her gaze went straight to his mouth. Some subconscious part of her wondered how his lips would feel against her own and the thought made her shiver. What was that about? Fear? Awareness? Weather-related? Darned if she knew. But the reaction told her she should refuse his deposit and tell him if the date opened up, she would let him know.

He met her gaze and assumed a puppy-dog expression to ratchet up his persuasion. "Kendra would be very disappointed."

Drat. That was the only thing he could have said to win her over. Thea couldn't let down a teenage girl whom she suspected had been let down one too many times already.

"All right, Scott. You win. I'll do the party."

He grinned again, showing his straight white teeth and very attractive smile. She thought of Little Red Riding Hood and the Big Bad Wolf and couldn't help feeling she'd just stepped alone into the woods on her way to Grandma's house.

Scott looked at his daughter biting into her enchilada. "Thanks for throwing dinner together, sweetie. I planned to get home early, but there was a problem at one of the sites."

"That's okay. Do you like it?" she asked, about the meal.

"It's great." And that was no lie. "When did you get to be such a good cook?"

"Thea gave me the recipe when she catered my friend's birthday party. She said it wasn't hard to make and almost impossible to mess up. I guess she was right."

Thea Bell. He'd had trouble getting her off his mind since leaving her office that morning. And that wasn't at all like him. He'd dated here and there, but nothing serious. And it had been a long time, so he wasn't used to thinking about a woman. Normally work was the only thing that took his mind off the ups and downs of his kids. But he'd found Thea was one smart cookie and pretty intuitive. She'd been right about the fact that he should listen to his daughter instead of lecturing.

But there was still the matter of that pregnancy test and it was too important to ignore. He so badly wanted to tell Kendra to do as he said, not as he'd done. He didn't want her to learn the same lessons he had learned in the school of hard knocks. But how could he get through to her? How would Thea approach this potential minefield?

He started to say there was something he wanted to talk to her about, then checked himself. That would be his daughter's signal to shut down.

He looked across the dinner table and decided to try a different tack. "This is nice. Having dinner together."

"Yeah. Nice." Warily, she met his gaze.

"I don't stop to appreciate it enough. And I should," he added.

"Why?"

"Lots of reasons. Because I enjoy spending time with you. And because when your sister was a baby, I hardly ever got to share a meal with the family."

"It's not that big a deal, Dad," she said. Her expression and tone told him she was ready to shut him down in a nanosecond if necessary.

"Yeah, it is. In those days, I was going to college at night and working during the day."

"But it's Grandad's company."

"That didn't mean I could slack off," he explained. "If anything, he was harder on me because we were related."

"I know the feeling," she muttered.

He refused to be sidetracked by even a mumbled verbal projectile. "The point is that between work and school, I put in a lot of hours away from home. It cost me time with you guys."

She pushed her plate away. "What are you really trying to say, Dad?"

So much for his different tack. He put his fork down. "Okay. Here's the deal. I made some choices that sent me on a path in life," he said, recalling what Thea had said. "I love you and your sister very much and wouldn't trade either of you for anything. But it was a path that took away my carefree youth. I don't want to see that happen to you."

She rolled her eyes. "Here we go."

"About the pregnancy test," he said. There was no subtle way to do this.

"I don't want to talk about it." She started to get up.

"Sit, Ken. I need to know. Was the test positive?"

"You saw the stick," she said, her hostility simmering. "Don't you know?"

"Thea said the results are inaccurate if it's been sitting for more than twenty minutes."

She'd known right off the top of her head what the stick was and how to interpret it. Along with the rules that would affect the damn plus or minus sign. He'd had no idea. It must be a female thing.

"Look, Dad, I really don't want to talk to you about this."

"Believe me, I don't like this any better than you. But I need to know if you're pregnant or not."

Her cheeks turned pink, and she stared down at her plate. "Not."

The weight he'd felt on his shoulders lifted and inside he was pumping his arm and hollering hallelujah with an exclamation point. Outside, he struggled not to react at all.

"Okay. That's good." Now part two of the conversation that was every father's worst nightmare. This was even worse than the birds and the bees talk that had led to an explanation of menstruation. At times like this, he was still angry as hell at his ex-wife for walking out. The hurt had disappeared long ago. But the resentment…he would carry that scar forever.

"The thing is, Ken, I'd have to be an idiot not to know you've had sex."

She looked at the table, refusing to meet his gaze. "I so don't want to talk to you about this. If you're going to force me to stay, can you just give me the Cliff's Notes on this lecture?"

"I'm not going to lecture," he said. "This is a dialogue."

"Meaning I have to talk?"

"That would make it less like a lecture," he pointed out. "Let me start by asking how you felt when you did the test."

She looked as if she wouldn't answer, then let out a sigh as she glanced up. "Scared," she admitted.

"I bet. Believe me, I understand. But you dodged a bullet. You get another chance to get it right. By 'it,' I mean birth control."

"I don't need another chance."

"If you think you're immune from the consequences of unprotected sex, I've got news for you—"

"I know, Dad. I got the message when my period was late."

"Then are we talking abstinence here?" he asked, his inner parent doing the dance of joy.

"Yes. I don't ever want to do 'it' again." Her eyes filled with tears.

He reached out and covered her hand with his own. It pleased him when she didn't pull away because he couldn't stand seeing her cry. Everything in him wanted to fix it—like he'd always done when she was a little girl. "What is it, Ken?"

"He was a creep. I can't believe I was so stupid."

"What?"

"In health class, the book said to use a condom because it's not only about not getting pregnant. I asked him to, but he said it doesn't feel as good. He said if I loved him I'd—" She met his gaze and said, "You know."

Yeah, he knew. Damn it all to hell, he knew. He tamped down the urge to put his fist through the wall. "So you did?"

She nodded, rubbing at a spot on the wood table with her thumb when she couldn't meet his gaze. "Then he dumped me. He went back to his girlfriend."

"Son of a bitch—" Anger swelled like a mushroom cloud inside him. "Who is he? Josh Hammond?"

"No. We broke up a long time ago. You don't know the guy."

"How can I not know him? I always screen your dates."

"Not always," she said.

He didn't have the reserves to deal with what he didn't know about his daughter. "I'll tear him apart. What's his name?"

"No way. I'm not telling you," she said, horrified. "I'd die. I'd have to go into the Witness Protection Program or something."

He blew out a long breath. "Okay. No names. For now. But you can't blame me for wanting to beat the crap out of him."

"I don't. But here's the thing, Dad. After I knew I wasn't pregnant, what bothered me most was how stupid I'd been. How I'd misjudged him."

"Don't feel like The Lone Ranger. I think that happens to everyone when a relationship goes south."

"Like you and Mom?"

He'd felt betrayed for putting everything he had into making it work when she couldn't have cared less.

After that, relationship abstinence looked pretty good. And still did.

"Yeah, like me and your mom."

Kendra shook her head as if she still didn't understand. "But I've known this guy since kindergarten. How could I have been so wrong? Worse, how can I trust my judgment ever again? How can I go to UCLA, which is like a small city, and tell the good guys from the bad ones?"

Scott felt the Aha! light come on. On top of what Thea had said about leaving the familiar behind, this was part of his daughter's problem with going away to school.

"You don't have to know," he said. "Don't trust any guy. And above all, don't sleep with any of them."

One corner of her mouth quirked up. "That doesn't help."

"It's good advice. Haven't you ever heard the only man a girl can trust is her dad?" He grinned. "Seriously, Ken, I've said this before. You shouldn't be—"

"Intimate until I'm in love or think I am," she quoted in a singsong voice. Who knew she'd been paying attention? "The problem is, I thought we were in love. I didn't know he wasn't." He opened his mouth to say something and she held up her hand. "Don't worry. The false alarm scared me. I'm never sleeping with a guy again."

He could tell her that in time she'd meet a nice guy who would appreciate the truly remarkable person she was. He could say that when she grew up, it would be easier to tell nice guys from the ones who were only after one thing. He could advise her not to judge all men by the one idiot. But he was a father, so he didn't.

He patted her hand and said, "My work here is done."

"Yeah, Dad," she said, and rolled her eyes. But she was smiling.

"I guess it's time to change the subject."

"Oh, yeah," she agreed.

"I have some news. I talked to Thea Bell this morning about catering your graduation party."

"And?" Her blue eyes brightened.

To see that sparkle back where it should be had been worth eating a little crow. And Thea had only poked a little fun at him. If her cooking went down as easily as that crow, it would be a great party. "She took the job. I gave her a check and signed a contract."

Kendra jumped up and threw her arms around his neck. "Thank you, Daddy. You won't regret it."

How could he regret anything that made her call him Daddy?

"I'm sure I won't."

She sat down and pulled her plate toward her. "Don't you just love Thea?"

Scott thought about the question and realized it was true. Not love; never again love. But he liked Thea. She was sweet, smart and sexy. Besides being all that and beautiful, too, she had an appealing sense of humor. And she was a widow. He realized that was all the 4-1-1 he had on the woman who knew so much about him.

He decided it would be a good idea to change that.

Several days later, Thea picked up the phone at her office desk to make a call when some movement on the sidewalk outside caught her attention. Her brain registered the fact that the strikingly good-looking man responsible was Scott Matthews. When her body got the message, her pulse and heart rate joined hands and started to boogie.

Boy, was she glad that Connie was in the back room. And that was silly because she would bet everything she owned that Scott wasn't any kind of physical threat. Which could only mean some part of her believed he was an emotional hazard and her partner's presence could prevent a meltdown.

He pushed open the door and walked inside. "Hi."

"Hi, yourself." She replaced the phone and noticed her hand was unsteady. Linking her fingers on top of her desk, she said, "To what do I owe this visit?"

Before he could respond, Connie walked into the front office. "T, I think we need to order—" She saw Scott and stopped. "Sorry. Is the dinger down? I didn't hear anyone come in."

Thea hadn't heard the dinger, either, because she couldn't hear a smart bomb go off over the blood pounding in her ears. So she ignored her partner's question.

She held her hand out indicating the man in front of them. "Meet Scott Matthews. He's the recently contracted client I told you about. Scott, this is my partner, Connie Howard."

Scott held out his hand. "Nice to meet you."

"You, too," Connie said, blatantly checking him out as she shook his hand. "Thea didn't tell me you were so—"

"How's Kendra?" Thea shot her friend a warning look. "That's his daughter. She's graduating from high school and the reason he's having the party we're doing."

"Right. The teenager." Connie leaned against the desk without taking her eyes off him.

He looked from Thea to Connie and shuffled his feet. "Kendra's fine."

"Connie, don't you have a cake to decorate back there?" Thea stared daggers.

The other woman stared back, then blinked and straightened. "Oh. Right. The Swanson shower. Bridal. Heart-shaped devil's food with raspberry filling. Seafoam-green icing."

When she was gone, Scott said, "Seafoam green?"

"The color of the bridesmaid's dresses."

"Ah." He nodded. "How dense of me."

"Yeah, I was going to say—" She shook her head as one corner of her mouth quirked up. Then she met his gaze. "How is Kendra *really?*"

"Not pregnant."

"I'm so glad," she said.

"Me, too."

"Was the conversation that produced this good news more listening or lecturing?" she asked.

"Half and half, I'd say. Actually when I shifted into lecture gear, she admitted she'd thought she was in love with the underhanded little twerp. He told her if she loved him she'd have sex without a condom."

"Oh, no!" Shocked, Thea put her hand over her mouth.

"Oh, yes. But after sleeping with her, he dumped my daughter and went back to his girlfriend. I'd like to clock the little weasel."

"Can I watch?"

His mouth curved up. "Unfortunately, Kendra swore me to nonviolence."

"Too bad."

"No kidding." He folded his arms over his chest. "What's worse, I think this is part of why she's dragging her feet about college. She got burned by a guy she's known practically all her life—"

"How can she trust herself with strangers?" Thea finished.

"Exactly."

"Poor kid."

"The silver lining is that she's never going to have sex again."

"You don't really believe that, do you?"

He sighed. "No. But if you're the charitable sort, don't give me a reality check for a while. This is my fantasy and I'd like to enjoy it for as long as possible."

"Okay." Thea laughed. "But I hope you told her that a man who really loves her wouldn't be as concerned with his own pleasure as much as protecting her."

"Actually, no. I was putting my testosterone to better use as I visualized the three hundred ways I planned to annihilate the little creep with my bare hands." He rubbed the back of his neck as he slid her a wry look. "Besides, I'm a little rusty in that department."

"Oh?" Did he mean sex? It was a lie. Had to be. A man as good-looking as Scott Matthews would have to beat women off with a stick. Surely he succumbed to physical temptation.

"Yeah. Between work and raising the girls, I haven't had the time or energy to be in the loop on this whole dating thing."

He looked charmingly sincere and her heart gave a funny little lurch at his admission. Women would fall at his feet, yet he'd channeled his energy into his children. How cool was that?

"So you're socially backward?"

"I guess you could say that." He chuckled and the sound was self-deprecating. "File me trying to advise my daughter under the blind leading the blind."

"Not entirely. You can clue her in on the male point of view."

"I guess that's something. And the next time we have

a heart-to-heart, I'll be sure to mention that the guy who really cares about her won't push her to do anything she's not comfortable with."

"You might also bring to her attention that it's one way to know her knight in shining armor as opposed to the knave who's simply using her." Thea shrugged. "It's also a way to know if that someone cares about her."

"Excellent point," he said. "Not only does Thea Bell toil for me. She's the guru of good sense, and I will pass that on to my offspring."

Thea smiled at him. His compliment produced a glow that had nothing to do with being pregnant. But it was familiar. She remembered falling in love with her husband. The ache inside when they were apart. The sheer giddiness when she saw him. The heart-pounding excitement. The anticipation of being together.

As she smiled up at Scott Matthews, her heart stuttered and her stomach fluttered. It occurred to her that this was very much like what she'd felt long ago.

But that was impossible.

Love like she'd had only happened once in a lifetime and she'd had hers.

"So what brings you here today?" she asked.

"The party. By the way, Kendra was very excited when I told her you'd be the caterer."

"I'm glad," she said. And she was. Until he moved closer.

Just like the last time he'd been here, he invaded her space and half sat on the corner of her desk. The pose pulled the denim tight across his leg, showcasing his muscular thigh. He folded his arms over his chest, in that oh-so-masculine way that drew attention to his above-average biceps. He was large and male and filled her personal area more than she was accustomed to it being filled. Or was it simply that he made her notice things she hadn't in a very long time?

She swallowed. "What about the party?"

"Have you had a chance to work up those figures for me on the cost yet?"

"I can't do it with any degree of accuracy because there are too many variables."

"Like what?"

"Number of guests. Choice of menu affects the cost of food. Theme impacts the price of decorations. You don't have to have a theme, of course. Although Kendra seemed excited about that. The two of you need to discuss it."

He nodded thoughtfully. "You mentioned that before. That day at the house."

"Right. I did."

If he remembered, why was he here? Until this moment the thought hadn't crossed her mind. She'd been too preoccupied with her reaction to him. He didn't have to drop by; he could have phoned to discuss this. Had he been looking for an excuse to see her face-to-face? She hoped not.

Why would he? By his own admission, he didn't have the time or energy for anything besides his work and his kids. And frankly, that was just fine with her. She was paddling the same canoe. Her work and her child-on-the-way were the focus of her world.

This was strictly business.

"Can you give me a ballpark figure?"

She thought about it. "I've done parties for a hundred dollars and some for over a thousand."

He whistled. "Whoa."

"It just depends. The cost of renting tables, chairs and linens is fixed, but without a number of people, it's meaningless information."

"I see."

"You should know that the cost of my labor is a good portion of the expense. Good caterers don't come cheap."

"I would never infer you were cheap," he said, raising an eyebrow.

"Good thing. Them's fightin' words."

"After all, you did say if you needed the gig that badly you wouldn't be considering a bigger house and a mortgage."

"True. And I have to tell you, your house fits my bill nicely."

"Have you listed your condo yet?"

"Yes. I'm hoping it will sell quickly, but Joyce said it's difficult to predict. Townhomes require a buyer with different criteria than single-family homes." Criteria like sending the last child off to college and downsizing. "Have you listed your house yet?"

"No. Kendra's reaction sort of put the brakes on that."

"I'm glad you're waiting. Maybe my place will sell and I can make an offer on yours."

"You liked it that much?"

"It's perfect, exactly what I was looking for. But we digress. Back to the party." And maybe there was another reason he was concerned about the cost. "Look, Scott, if money is a problem—"

He held up his hand. "I can afford you. But there's no harm in negotiating."

"Depends on the terms."

"If the cost of labor is the only variable, I say we start there."

"But I already know how much your daughter wants me to do the party."

"And I know how much you like my house." He grinned.

The smile was so devastating, it made her glad she was already sitting. "Did I tip my hand?" she managed to ask.

"Big-time."

"I didn't peg you for the wheeler-dealer type."

"I'm a wolf in sheep's clothing."

Her thoughts exactly.

He stared at her for several moments, and she could almost see the mental wheels turning. "How about this? I'll hold off on listing the house until there's an offer on your condo if you agree to discount your labor costs for the party?"

She thought about his suggestion. Basically, she would be trading her time for an insurance policy to have first crack at his house. Considering how much she liked the place, how perfect it would be for her needs and the fact that she knew it might get snapped up before she could sell her place, she figured it was a cheap insurance policy.

"I think you've got yourself a deal, Mr. Matthews." She held out her hand.

He took it in his big, warm palm and gave her a firm squeeze. "Glad to hear it, Ms. Bell."

When he released her hand, the palm tingled where he'd held it. And her cheeks felt warm. If there was a God in heaven, she wasn't blushing like a schoolgirl. For Pete's sake, his teenage daughter probably wouldn't redden like this simply because a man touched her.

She hated feeling out of her depth and less than in control. Too many things in life were uncontrollable, she'd learned. She should be able to deal with a man. But Scott Matthews wasn't like any man she'd ever met. And they'd just struck a bargain. She couldn't help thinking she'd just made a deal with the big, bad wolf. Except he'd said he wasn't and she believed him. Somehow that was so much worse.

He looked down at her. "So you're a widow."

The big, bad wolf had just stepped out of his sheep's clothing.

Chapter Five

Smooth move, Matthews, he thought.

He hadn't planned to blurt that out, but starting a conversation required personal information. The fact that she was a widow was all he had. On top of that, lack of dating experience put him at a distinct disadvantage. "What's your sign?" wasn't something he said to start up a meaningful dialogue with a woman. And he found he very much wanted to do that with Thea. But he didn't want it to be about catering, kids or real estate contracts.

He kicked himself when his thoughtless remark turned her cocoa-colored eyes dark. And sad. She'd never said how long she'd been a widow, and he felt like the world's biggest jerk.

"I'm sorry," he said. "I didn't mean to bring up bad memories."

"That's all right. I've had time to deal with it."

"How long ago did you lose your husband?"

"David died two years ago."

At least it hadn't been two weeks ago. That made him feel marginally better. "What happened? If you don't mind my asking."

"Actually, I don't really like to talk about it." She stood up. "I try to keep my personal and professional life separate, Scott. You're in business. I'm sure you understand."

"Yeah." But he didn't really. She'd shut him down faster than a roofing crew in an electrical storm.

He also didn't understand what it was like to lose a spouse. His was alive and well somewhere—just not with him and the girls. Thea's husband was gone for good. The shadows lingering in her eyes told him she'd cared about the guy a lot. Or did she look like that because she thought Scott was trying to hit on her?

He'd told her he was out of practice. Hell, he'd never really been *in* practice. He'd been a family man when his high school buddies were perfecting their pick-up lines. He'd never had a chance to use his—"Hi, I'm Scott. How do you like me so far?" He took one look at her face and decided this wasn't the best time to take it out for a test drive. Besides, she barely knew him. She had no reason to trust him. But he wanted her to.

"Look, Thea, through a weird twist of fate, you were there for me at a very difficult time. As I recall, you said you'd never met a person who looked more like they needed to talk."

"Yes, but—"

"I could say the same about you. You told me—and I quote—'Talking is helpful.' I'd like to return the favor."

She smiled, but it didn't push the clouds from her eyes. "I appreciate that, Scott. But there's really nothing to say. It's in the past. I've dealt with it. But thanks for the offer."

"Any time. I owe you one."

"No. Really." She looked at her desk calendar. "But we do need to talk about details for your daughter's party. When is good for you?"

"Evenings are best."

"I figured. What about tomorrow?" She looked up and met his gaze.

"It's Friday," he said, trying to remember if he had anything going on with the girls.

"Of course. The beginning of the weekend. You've got plans."

He shook his head. "I don't think so. My social calendar isn't exactly on PowerBook. But sometimes Gail comes home from college for the weekend. To do laundry."

"Not to see you?" She grinned.

The unexpected smile hit him between the eyes and jump-started his pulse. She should do that more often. It was like seeing the sun peek out from behind thick cloud cover. Not only did it chase away the lingering shadows, but it made her look so beautiful she took his breath away.

He couldn't help smiling back. "I used to think so, but I got real when I figured out she spent more time with the washer and dryer than she did telling me about her classes and friends."

Thea laughed. "I'm sure she misses you."

"You don't have to say that. I'm a father. I no longer have an ego. Tomorrow night is fine. Do you want me to meet you here?"

She thought for a moment. "How about if I meet you at the house? That way if your daughter is there, you don't have to leave."

"Great."

"I'll be there at seven, if that's okay?"

"Should be."

Scott said his goodbyes and walked outside. He was looking forward to Friday night in a way he hadn't since he'd been a teenager with a brand-new driver's license.

Thea stood to the side of the window where she couldn't be seen and watched Scott's truck pull out of the parking lot. When he merged into the traffic on Valencia Boulevard, she breathed a sigh of relief.

"He's quite a hunk."

At the sound of Connie's voice, Thea whirled and splayed her hand over her chest. "You scared me."

"You should be scared. But not because of me. Thea," she said, tsking as she shook her head. "Tall. Dark. Blue eyes? Your description of him is as bland as unseasoned sirloin. And I repeat—be afraid, very afraid."

"Why?"

"The man practically issued an engraved invitation and you shut him down like a lid on a grease fire."

"Were you eavesdropping?" Thea asked, putting her hands on her hips.

"Of course." Connie didn't look the least bit repentant. "And spying."

"So we were listening to the same conversation?"

"Yes. And drooling over the same hunk."

"I wasn't drooling."

Connie met her gaze. "Okay. But this time, I'm absolutely sure there's a sparkle in your eyes. And after meeting Scott, I know the reason for it."

"Let's get back to the engraved invitation. What exactly would you be referring to? An invitation to what?" Thea asked.

look seemed to take it up a notch. There was something about a man and his tool belt that set a woman's hormones bubbling and boiling.

"H-hi." Her voice sounded breathless and she hoped he would think it was the trek up the driveway.

"Hi. Come in." He closed the door. "I'm sorry. I just got home. There was a shortage of manpower at one of the construction sites and I filled in."

"A boss who's not afraid to get his hands dirty," she observed.

"And the rest of him, too," he said ruefully. "Look, I'm going to take a quick shower. I'll just be a few minutes. Make yourself comfortable. The girls are in the other room. Kendra will introduce you to Gail," he finished, just before he disappeared upstairs.

On her way through the living room and dining room, Thea heard female voices and giggling. Kendra and another girl were lounging on the corner group in the family room.

"Hi," she said, looking at both girls.

"Thea." Kendra stood. "I didn't know you were coming over."

"Your dad didn't tell you?"

"I've sort of been avoiding him." She looked at the other girl. "This is my sister Gail."

"Nice to meet you, Thea," she said standing.

The older sister was the same height as Kendra, but her hair was lighter and shot with gold streaks. Her big green eyes sparkled with intelligence and were frankly assessing.

"My pleasure, Gail. I've heard a lot about you. All good." Thea winked at Kendra. "Your dad said you were happy about me doing the party."

She grinned. "I am."

"Good. I'm here to help you make some decisions so I can give him an estimate of expenses."

"Great. Gail's home for the weekend." She glanced at her sister. "She's good at the creative part."

"Not the food," she clarified. "But other stuff. I was on the decorating committee for my sorority. I've done a party or two."

Thea nodded. "Good. That's not my strongest area. I like the food part."

She studied the two sisters, side by side, and remembered when she'd first met Kendra at her friend's catered birthday party. While Thea had set up, the teen had asked a lot of questions. Was it hard to cook? How had she learned? Who taught her? Did she like it?

Thea had enjoyed spending time with her that day. She wondered if the child she carried was a girl and thought how lovely it would be to share her interest in cooking, clothes and other girlie things. She'd sensed something needy in Kendra when she'd first met her. Now that she knew her history, it didn't take a Ph.D. in psychology to get that it was about missing her mother. Anger curled through her toward the woman who'd deserted her daughters. It was reprehensible. There was no way to come out of that without feeling the effects.

Her baby would never know its father and nothing could change that. It made her sad, but there was nothing to be done except give her child all the love and attention she had in her. Plus the best environment to bring up her baby. She looked around and knew without a doubt that she liked this house even more the second time.

She heard the water go on upstairs. An instant visual of a shirtless Scott Matthews jumped into her mind. Her stomach lurched and she wished it was about the pregnancy. Why had she volunteered to come here? She looked at Kendra and remembered.

"So," she said, "why are you avoiding your dad?"

The teen glanced at her sister, but before she could say anything Gail spoke up. "There's an overnight freshman orientation coming up that he wants Ken to go to."

"And you don't want to?" Thea asked.

"He's just trying to get rid of me."

"Oh, for Pete's sake, Ken," her sister said. "Dad's not doing that. You're just a big chicken."

"You're afraid?" Thea asked.

"No." Her mouth took on a stubborn slant, remarkably like her father's.

"You should give it a try," Thea advised.

"What if it's lame?" Kendra looked up and for just a moment there was apprehension in the blue-eyed gaze she'd also inherited from Scott.

"What if it's not?" Thea sat on the arm of the wing chair in the family room. "You've got nothing to lose by checking it out. That's what orientation is all about."

"You've been talking to my dad, haven't you?"

"Yes," Thea admitted. "But not about this. I'm not taking his side if that's what you're implying. It simply makes good sense."

"Why?"

"You get a taste of what college life will be like. You do want to go, right?"

"Of course."

"You have an opportunity to go to one of the most prestigious colleges in the country. UCLA is an excellent school and it's practically in your backyard. You're far enough away to get a taste of being on your own, but close enough if you need—" she glanced at Gail "—laundry facilities."

"Is that what my dad told you?" she asked, grinning.

"He actually said that when you come home, you spend more time with the washer and dryer than you do with him."

Just then a buzzer sounded from down the hall. Gail rubbed her nose sheepishly. "Right on cue. That would mean my darks are done." She left the room to tend to her clothes.

Thea laughed. "He wasn't complaining. Just stating a fact. You're growing up," she said, looking at Kendra. "And he wants you to have the best possible education. What if you like it?"

"What if I don't?" the teen asked.

"Then you can enroll at the local junior college. There's more than one way to get from point A to point B. But don't limit yourself because you're afraid."

"I'm not afraid," she said. "Just a little nervous. It's a big place."

Thea remembered what Scott had said about doubting her ability to judge people after her unfortunate experience. She knew it would embarrass the teen to know that she knew. Instead of bringing it up, she said, "It *is* a big place. That can work in your favor. Makes it easy to blend in. To not be noticed. Has it occurred to you that you're not the only freshman who feels this way? There will be a whole crop of newbies feeling just as insecure as you do."

"Yeah," she said a little doubtfully.

Thea put her hand on the girl's arm. "Just don't let fear stop you. Take the steps. Your dad will be there to catch you if you fall."

Kendra shrugged. "I've always hated the first day of school. Especially in elementary school. Not knowing which teacher I'd get—would she be nice or the Wicked Witch of the West."

Elementary school. It would come in handy for her child. She would check out the school system. But this was an opportunity to get information from someone who'd walked the hallowed halls.

"What did you think of your elementary school?" Thea asked her.

She thought for a moment. "It was good. I liked it."

Thea couldn't resist. "A few years from now you could be saying that about UCLA."

"Maybe." Kendra grinned. "When I was in grade school, I remember a lot of the parents would ask for their kids to be with certain teachers, but my dad never did."

"Why's that?"

"He said in life you don't get to pick people. You have to learn how to get along with anyone and everyone, no matter what."

Very practical, Thea thought. "So overall you'd say your experience in elementary school was positive?"

Scott walked into the room. "What's this about school?"

"I was just asking your daughter about her experience. When one is interested in the educational system, one should go to the person who's walked the walk."

"Why are you interested?" He folded his arms over his chest.

This wasn't the time to share that she was concerned about the future education of the child she was carrying. But she also couldn't ignore him or blow off the question. So she seized the only thing she could think of. "Have you forgotten our deal?"

"No."

"Okay, then. It's something any prospective buyer should be aware of. One should always be concerned about resale. And the school system is important in that regard."

"It was one of my concerns," he agreed.

"What deal?" Kendra looked at her. "Are you going to buy the house?"

Uh-oh. She'd stepped right on that land mine. She didn't want to make things more difficult for Scott, but she also wouldn't lie to the girl.

"I'm looking for a bigger place and I love this house. But I have to sell my condo first and that could take a while. So your dad agreed to hold off on listing the house until my condo sells and give me first crack at making an offer on this house."

Kendra nodded. "Cool."

Thea looked at Scott, who was staring at his daughter as if she was an alien from another planet. "Cool?" he said.

"Yeah." She cocked her thumb toward the laundry. "I'm going to help Gail."

"Okay." Scott stared after her, scratching his head with a puzzled expression on his face.

The scent of soap and some spicy cologne tickled Thea's nose and she looked at him. His damp hair was darker and showed marks where he'd run his comb through the wet strands. He'd put on fresh jeans and a black T-shirt that clung to his flat abdomen and the impressive contours of his chest. The muscles in his upper arms flexed and rippled as he rubbed the back of his neck. She'd forgotten how good a man looked and smelled fresh out of the shower. A feeling of longing sliced through her, making the empty place inside her echo with the pain of what would never be.

"Just the other day she had a meltdown about selling the house. Now it's 'cool'? I will never understand the complexity of the female mind," he said, the corners of his mouth curving up.

The bemused look was so darn cute. Thea felt a tug in the region of her heart, and it chased away the yearning she'd felt just a moment ago. How could this happen? She was the one who'd planted both feet solidly on her soapbox while delivering the lecture about keeping her personal and professional lives separate. She didn't need a visit from the common-sense fairy to know it was time to do what she came here to do and then beat a hasty retreat.

"So what kind of food did you have in mind for the party?" she asked Scott. "What does Kendra like?"

"Chicken," called out a voice from the other room that belonged to Gail. Good-natured chatter followed the remark.

When Thea laughed, Scott looked puzzled. "Apparently I missed something."

"Not important." She picked up her briefcase and walked to the kitchen dinette to open it. She took out an album of pictures from parties she'd done. After opening it, she stopped at a page. "This is a party I did with Greek food. But it was for a wedding shower and the couple was going to Greece for their honeymoon. And the bride was a vegetarian."

He nodded as he studied the pictures. "I'm trying to remember if I was ever that young."

"I know what you mean," she said. "But it was not my intention that you get philosophical on me. My purpose in showing these is to demonstrate how theme can complement the menu—and any dietary idiosyncrasies."

"As long as there's meat." He arched an eyebrow at her.

The girls walked into the room, Gail carrying a basket filled with folded clothes. "Dad, Ken and I are thinking about going to a movie."

You're leaving us alone? What's wrong with you? Thea wanted to shout at them. But she managed to hold back.

"Kendra, don't you want to be in on the menu discussion?" she asked instead.

"You're the one who wanted this party in the first place," Scott said. "I thought you'd want to help plan it."

"You didn't tell me Thea was coming over," she defended.

"Okay. But I thought this party was important to you. Now that she's here, the least you can do is hang around and tell her what you want."

"But Gail and I don't get to spend a lot of time hanging out together."

"Tell me about it," he said.

Gail set down the overflowing laundry basket. "What about a balloon theme? Something like, 'The sky's the limit.'"

Scott glanced at Thea. "Are balloons expensive?"

"Depends on how many you have and if they're the Mylar ones filled with helium. But you can do a few of those and some you blow up yourself."

He nodded. "Then I think it's a brilliant idea."

"Dad, you squeeze a penny till it shrieks," Gail needled.

"Someone around here has to be frugal," he defended. "You guys think money grows on trees."

"It doesn't?" Kendra said, eyes wide as she glanced from him to her sister.

Scott reached over and tweaked her nose. "Very funny."

"I think it's a brilliant idea, too," Thea agreed. "So we have a theme. What about food? Anything ethnic you're particularly fond of?"

"Mexican," Gail said.

"Oriental," Kendra chimed in.

Scott looked at them. "Steak and baked potatoes."

"Anyone can do that," Kendra pointed out. "Thea's food is special."

"So what do you want?" he asked.

"To go to the movies with my sister."

"But Thea gave up her evening to come over here."

She hadn't given up much, she thought. Just her empty condo and a frozen dinner. "Don't worry about it, Scott."

"It's not about worrying. It's about inconveniencing people," he said, giving the girls a stern look.

"But they didn't know I was coming. Besides, you guys can't even agree on what kind of food you want." She tapped her lip. "I think I have a suggestion that might help."

"What?" he asked, sounding doubtful.

"Why don't I come back at a mutually convenient time for everyone and we'll do a tasting to see what you like." She watched the three of them nod. "I'll pick some dishes that have received the most positive feedback—"

"No pun intended," Scott said.

"Right." She grinned. "I'll cook and maybe we can pin down the food. What do you say?"

"Are you sure you don't mind coming back?" he asked.

Of course she did, but not for the reasons he thought.

But now she was in for a penny, in for a pound. And she wouldn't let Kendra down.

"It's fine. That way the girls can go to the movies and hang out."

Scott let out a long breath. "I suppose it's all right since we're just in the discussion stage."

The girls stood on either side of him and kissed him on each cheek. "Thanks, Dad," they said in unison.

Gail put her laundry basket by the stairway, while Kendra picked up her keys and purse. Then they were gone and the energy level dropped. But when Thea looked at Scott, the level of something else went up.

"So when are you coming back to cook for me?" he asked. "How about next Thursday? You just got a crash course in how complicated weekends are around here."

She nodded and checked her date book. "That works for me."

And the words were barely out of her mouth before her anticipation to see him again set in. That did not work for her.

Chapter Six

He'd seen women more beautiful, but Scott couldn't remember who or when.

Thea was standing in front of his stove, about where he'd seen her for the very first time. Now she was wearing jeans, a soft fuzzy green sweater that brought out hints of hazel in her big brown eyes and an apron with her catering logo—For Whom The Bell Toils. The "O" in *Toils* was in the shape of a bell and the dinger looked like a wooden spoon. It was catchy. And, like her, it was cute, clever and captivating.

She glanced at him over her shoulder as she sprinkled grated mozzarella cheese over lasagna noodles. "Scott, I can call you when everything is ready for you to taste."

Right. The party menu. The reason she was here. Pretty soon he'd get his head into making a decision on that, but right now all he could think about was tasting the comely caterer.

"Scott?" Her hand hovered above the baking dish as she studied him with a puzzled expression. "Is something wrong?"

"Nope. Everything is peachy." He took a drink from the beer in his hand. "Are you sure you wouldn't like a glass of wine? I've got a nice bottle of cabernet. Been saving it for a special occasion."

She turned back to the stove. "I've learned never to mix work and wine unless it's called for in a recipe."

"Probably wise," he said.

"This will take at least a half hour to heat through. I would have put it together at the office, but the luncheon I did today ran a little late."

"No problem," he said. "It's exciting to stand around and watch the cheese melt."

"Ah. Sarcasm." One corner of her full mouth tilted up. "So don't stand around. Go watch the grass grow or the car rust. The cheese will melt whether you're here or not. You must have something better to do than hang around with me."

"Not really. For a change it's kind of nice to not be the one cooking." At the moment, he couldn't think of anything he'd rather do than watch her. "So what have you brought to taste? Besides the lasagna?"

"I have a Greek salad," she said indicating a bowl of greens on the counter. "Some egg rolls I made from scratch. They're left over from the luncheon today and they're really good if I do say so myself. I assembled quesadillas—they're simple—tortillas and cheese—but if you like them and want more pizzazz, I can use salsa, guacamole and beans. Jalapeño peppers can spice them up and make them hotter."

He could think of ways to spice things up he thought,

staring at her mouth. And that definitely made him hotter.

"Sounds like you've put together a veritable United Nations for the palate."

"I like that," she said with a grin. "And once we have an ethnic direction, I can narrow down your choices and fine-tune the recipes, taking into consideration your personal preferences. Also, you don't have to stick with just Italian or Mexican food. You can mix and match if you want."

"That wouldn't be breaking any catering code?"

Her eyes sparkled. "None I'm aware of. Some clients like to stick with one direction, but it's not carved in stone. It all depends on what you want. The customer is always right." She stuck her hands in the pockets of her apron. "Seriously, if you have something you need to do, I'll just let you know when everything is ready."

That was the third time she'd hinted he should hit the road and get out from underfoot. Did he make her nervous? Or was she a temperamental chef who didn't like anyone peeking over her shoulder? He sort of liked that he might make her nervous—if it wasn't nervous in the "temperamental cook" kind of way. If it was the sort of nerves that meant she was as aware of him as he was of her, he could go for that.

"Don't worry about me," he said. "I can take care of myself."

"I'm not worried. You're a big boy," she said, not quite meeting his gaze. "Where's Kendra? I haven't seen her."

It was a natural question, considering the fact that his daughter had initiated this whole thing in the first place. But it was the way Thea had asked, as if she were hoping. As if *she* were worried—about being alone with him.

"She's at a friend's house."

"But she was supposed to be here."

Scott shrugged. "I know. Something came up for school. I was going to call and cancel but she talked me out of it." And that had taken precious little effort.

"I see." She tapped her lip. "When will she be home?"

"Ten at the latest. That's her curfew on school nights."

"Hmm." Thea met his gaze. "It would be nice to get her input. Since this party is for her. And that's why I came back."

"She said everything you make is to die for—that's a direct quote—and I should pick what I like." His gaze zeroed in on the slender column of Thea's neck, which he liked very much. He noticed her pulse fluttering and his own kicked up to keep pace.

"Okay." She nodded. "She can reheat the leftovers and let me know what she thinks. Often they're better because the flavors have time to blend. But I have to warn you, if there's anything you love and she hates it, her opinion as guest of honor carries the most weight."

"Even though I'm paying the bill?" He couldn't resist teasing her. Maybe he could shake her out of this stiff, professional pose. If he'd never seen her sympathetic-listener side, he wouldn't miss it now. But he had and he did.

"You're paying the bill because you love your daughter and want her to be happy."

"You're sure about that?"

"Absolutely," she said, nodding emphatically.

"I'm that transparent?"

"Like plastic wrap."

"You've learned all my secrets," he confirmed.

"Then my work here is done." But her gaze skittered away. She pointed at the clutter on the refrigerator beside him. "Does it always look like that?"

He studied the mass of magnets, some of them with clips holding coupons, school memos and pictures. "Yeah, pretty much."

She tapped her lip. "I can't decide if it's a fire hazard or a work of art."

"Probably both," he said with a grin.

She plucked off a magnetic frame with a photo in it. "Which one of the girls is this?"

He moved in close to look, even though he knew exactly which one of his daughters it was. "That's Kendra. She was three months old."

Gently, she traced the picture with her finger, as if it were a real, live baby. "She's so sweet."

As sweet as you smell, he thought breathing in her floral scent. A soft, tender look crept into Thea's face as she studied the small photo. He hadn't thought she could look more beautiful, but she did. It took all his willpower to keep from reaching out to trace the curve of her cheek and the line of her jaw. The skin there looked incredibly soft and smooth and perfect. Her small nose turned up slightly with a dusting of freckles splashed over it.

Strands of hair shimmered around her face like brown silk. It was all he could do to keep from tangling his fingers in it and pulling her to him to taste her mouth, see if it was made for kissing as he suspected. The sight of her made his chest tight and for the first time in a long time, he felt the emptiness inside.

"She's completely adorable." Thea looked at him. "I can't believe you know exactly how old she is in this picture."

"Besides the fact that it's written on the back," he said, "I remember everything. I've been involved in all my girls' activities—Indian princesses, sports, school."

"Did work get in the way of being a father?" she asked wryly.

"Sometimes. But since my dad owns the company, it was a little easier to juggle my time. Any pressure about work came from me trying not to take advantage."

"So much for trying to make me believe you're a tough guy where your daughter is concerned." She looked around the kitchen and into the family room. "Your girls practically grew up in this house. For a man who remembers everything, doesn't that make you think twice about selling it?"

He shrugged as he followed her gaze. "It's just a house. The memories are up here," he said, tapping his temple. "I've got a ton of pictures, ninety-nine-point-nine percent of which are *not* in albums. I wish digital cameras had been around when my girls were growing up."

"Digital cameras?" she asked, a spark in her eyes.

"Yeah. The technology makes storing the memories easier and that appeals to me. Are you interested?" He looked into her eyes and wished they were talking about something more personal than the latest photo technology. Then he realized how his question might sound and added, "In cameras?"

"Yes. I'm going to need a good one for—" She stopped, looking uncomfortable. "F-for business. I like to take photos of my parties," she said quickly.

"I remember. We looked at them the other night when you were here."

"Right," she said, nodding emphatically. "But I'm not into technology much. Connie keeps trying to get me to join the twenty-first century, but my heels are dug in and I'm hanging on to the past with both hands."

He laughed. "In certain things I can understand that."

"Meaning?"

"I've tried my damnedest to keep my girls from growing up. But apparently they didn't get the memo that they're supposed to stay small."

"So you do have mixed feelings about your daughter leaving home and selling the place."

"Yes. But soon I'll rattle around this big house. It's time for something smaller."

Looking unconvinced, she leaned back and studied him. "Fibber. I think you're a big softie."

Shaking his head, he said, "No way. I'm hard as nails and practical. It's going to be quiet and peaceful around here. When Kendra goes to college, the phone won't be ringing off the hook and the energy level will drop to normal proportions."

"*If* she goes away."

"Even if she decides on the local junior college for now, I'm looking at two years tops until she transfers to a four-year school. The handwriting is on the wall. She's going to leave whether or not I want her to and I'll need a smaller place."

"And when you're alone, you're going to miss her— teen problems and all."

He scoffed. "I'll miss her. But after recent events, I will never miss teenage problems."

Thea looked down at the picture in her hands and smiled, softly—sadly. Why sad? What was she thinking to make her look like that?

He wanted to know. And it hit him like a two-by-four to the head—he wanted to fix whatever was bothering her. But he couldn't do that without knowing what was wrong. Only the last time he'd tried to draw her out, she'd refused to cooperate. Should he try again? The answer was yes, although not tonight. He didn't want to give her a reason to hide behind her professional demeanor. Or worse, head for the hills. He was enjoying her company too much.

He felt a click with her and suspected she felt it, too. He'd admit to being out of practice with women. His experiences were few and far between, but he didn't remember feeling an attraction like this before. Even if he wanted to, a man couldn't forget a woman like her.

Thea put the magnetic frame back on the refrigerator. "So you're absolutely and completely committed to getting a smaller place?"

"Yup. Like I said—hard as nails and practical. What do I need with this big house just for me?"

"What if the girls want to come home for a visit?"

"I'm not going to live in a cardboard box under the freeway. Wherever I move will just be smaller, but I'll want a couple of extra bedrooms."

One of her delicate eyebrows arched. "I happen to know of a place like that."

"Oh?"

"Yeah. My condo." Before he could say anything, she rushed on. "Actually it was Connie's idea. I told her you were downsizing and, being Connie, she said in her flippant way that maybe we should trade spaces."

Scott rested his forearm on the refrigerator, leaning in close to look down at her. "Intriguing idea."

"Isn't it?" She blinked as she gazed up at him and swallowed. "She actually called it brilliant, but humility has never been her most attractive quality."

"I hadn't gotten as far as thinking where I'd move to, but a condo makes a lot of sense."

"It's practical," she said, lifting that eyebrow again.

"Have I mentioned I'm a practical guy?"

"No way," she said in mock surprise.

"Yeah." He grinned.

"Then you should check out my place and see if you're interested."

He was interested all right. Checking out her mouth, he felt the blood flow in his body shift to points south of his belt. Some rusty instinct warned him that this wouldn't be the best time to check out if her lips were as soft and sexy as they looked. Not if he wanted to know her better. And since she'd just given him a gold-plated invitation to do just that, he could wait.

"I'd like very much to see your place."

"Great. Let's look at our calendars and we'll set up a time."

He could hardly wait.

A week after her visit to Scott's house, Thea looked at the clock on her microwave. He was due any minute. Instantly, the threads of nerves in her stomach tied into one gigantic knot.

At this moment, and every one since the words had come out of her mouth, she wished for the invitation back. She was as tense as a chef watching a soufflé. Which was silly because this was business. Sort of. He had a big place and needed a smaller one. She had a smaller one and needed a bigger one. Simply business.

But it felt very personal and complicated, which made her uneasy.

The doorbell sounded and she pressed a palm against her abdomen as the knot grew. She glanced in the peephole to check to make sure it was Scott. It was. And even distorted by the peephole, just as Connie had said, he was female-fantasy material. Not for her, of course. But the average woman would be putty in his hands.

Bracing herself, she turned the dead bolt. With her practiced, professional smile firmly in place, she opened the door. "Scott. I'm glad you could make it."

"Me, too." He walked in and smiled.

"You're right on time."

She shut the door after him, then turned to find him looking around. He'd walked the length of her entry and waited to step down into her great room. As always, her gaze was drawn to his impressive physique, and it occurred to her that this was the first time she'd seen him in something other than jeans and work boots. In his khaki slacks and the navy knit shirt molded to his broad shoulders, muscular back and trim waist, he cleaned up pretty good. She marveled at her instantaneous female response to that realization. It was nice to know that part of her still worked. Nice, but nerve-racking. In order to avoid more of the same, she resolved to suck it up and get this over with.

She looked up at him. "I'll show you around."

"Okay."

With her arm out, she indicated the long kitchen with a nook at the end where her dinette sat. "This is where For Whom the Bell Toils was born."

"I can see why you lease an office. It doesn't have a lot of counter space."

"Is that a problem for you?"

"On the contrary," he said. "Less is more as far as I'm concerned."

"This is my living room. There's my office where I do paperwork," she said, indicating the room set off with French doors. "It could be a downstairs bedroom if you wanted. Although, obviously a solid door would need to be there."

He grinned. "I'm a builder. Doors are my domain."

"Oh. Right. Of course. That would be a piece of cake for you." She indicated the stairway. "I'll show you the upstairs."

"The last time we did this, there were surprises." He held out his arm for her to precede him. "You go first."

"I guarantee there's nothing to be afraid of," she teased.

"I'm not taking any chances."

She led him up, past where the stairs turned, opening to a loft on the left. Through double doors, she took him into her bedroom. "It's spacious. Big, walk-in closet, double sinks, separate stall shower."

"Nice," he said, looking around.

She'd chosen roses and ruffles for her bedroom. The walls were painted a neutral rosy beige color and there were vases of dried flowers and a dish of potpourri on her nightstand. It couldn't be more feminine. And he couldn't possibly look more masculine and out of place in her froufrou space. The thought was like a speed bump to her racing heart and just as surely it shook her up.

"There are two more bedrooms." As he looked in, she swallowed the breathlessness she'd heard in her voice. When she felt in control, she said, "These would make perfect guest rooms for Gail and Kendra when they come to visit."

He met her gaze and the corners of his mouth turned up. "I can see why you're such a busy caterer. Never miss an opportunity to market your product."

She shrugged. "I'm not doing a sales presentation. It's the truth."

When they were back downstairs, she wasn't sure what to do. Should she ask him to sit down? Offer him a drink? At his place it had thrown her when he'd offered her a glass of wine. If she hadn't been pregnant, she'd have been tempted to take it. That reaction had unnerved her. She was the businesswoman; he was the client. But with Scott, the line between business and pleasure blurred. Something sizzled between them that fried the professional parameters and turned the politically correct into soot.

But she'd been taught that you could never go wrong being polite. Her mother's voice in her head wouldn't let her be anything less. Maybe he had to get home and would turn her down. "I'm sorry I don't have any beer. Would you like a glass of iced tea? Or a soda?"

"Iced tea would be great."

She should have known. But since she'd opened her big mouth again and made the offer, she couldn't very well take it back. If only she didn't feel the power of his appeal every time they were in the same room.

She walked into her kitchen and reached into the cupboard beside the refrigerator for a glass. After putting in some ice, she pulled out the tea pitcher and poured. "Would you like lemon and sugar?"

He shook his head and took the drink. After sipping, he looked at the glass, then at her. "What flavor is that?"

"Passion fruit."

As soon as the words were out of her mouth, she blushed like a teenager. She hadn't blushed this much around a guy even when she *was* a teenager.

To his credit, he didn't say anything except, "It's really good."

She leaned her back against the counter. "Town house living is ideal for a busy professional like yourself."

"How so?"

"Outside maintenance is taken care of by an association. I have a small yard in back—patio large enough for a barbecue and a bit of grass and flowers. But essentially there's no upkeep."

"Good to know."

"It's important information to have when one is phasing out responsibility."

"That's something impossible for a father to escape. With two kids in college I'm looking at mega-obligations for a long time to come. And if either of the girls wants to go for a master's degree, I'll be doing dad duty even longer." He lifted one broad shoulder. "I'm just looking to simplify my living arrangements."

Thea understood that. This town house was where she'd moved to escape the painful memories after her husband died. It became her haven, allowed her to uncomplicate her life. Now she was ready to take on the responsibility of being a mother. She ached with the need to hold her baby in her arms.

She looked at Scott and said sincerely, "This is the perfect place to simplify your lifestyle. It's a little over twenty-three hundred square feet, by the way. Big, but not too big. Just the right amount of space without being overwhelming."

He set his empty glass on the counter. "You're preaching to the choir. I like your place. A lot. It's exactly what I need."

When he said the last words, his gaze darkened with intensity as he looked at her mouth. The realization made her skin grow warm and put a hitch in her breathing. She felt as if she needed to suck in air, yet she couldn't manage to because of the tightness in her chest.

She cleared her throat. "Maybe it's something we should pursue. The real-estate deal, I mean."

He nodded. "I agree."

"I'll call Joyce. If you're serious about swapping spaces, maybe she can cut us a break on her commission. This deal would be half the work."

"Maybe." The soles of his loafers scraped on her tile floor as he shifted his weight. "We can look into that. But—"

"Yes?" she asked eagerly, excited at the prospect of buying his house. It was everything she wanted. A kitchen large enough to do a lot of her work in, as well as being in the school district where she wanted her son or daughter educated. The perfect place to raise her child. And, she thought, the house had a positive parental vibe. She would be living in the same place as the man who'd successfully raised two fine young women.

He jammed his hands into his pockets as he shifted his feet. "There's something I'd like to ask you."

"Okay." He looked nervous. What was that about?

"Would you have dinner with me sometime?"

Dinner? To talk things over? Just the two of them? Not a good idea. "That's very nice of you, Scott. But it's not necessary for you to take me out to dinner to discuss real estate details."

He shook his head. "Actually, talking business was the furthest thing from my mind. I meant I'd like to take you out for a meal and discuss anything *but* business."

"You mean a date?"

"Yeah." His expression went from tense to sheepish. "But if you have to ask, I guess I'm way rustier at this whole thing than I realized."

He wasn't the only one. If she was more with it, she'd have seen this coming, but she hadn't.

"No." She shook her head. "Dinner's out of the question."

He stared at her with a puzzled expression. "The last time I checked, dinner was a meal that most people take for granted they're going to eat."

Drat. He wasn't going to let it drop. But a date simply wasn't going to happen. And she couldn't violate her prime directive to explain why. She refused to talk about her baby yet. Call her superstitious, but it felt like asking for trouble—a challenge to the fates.

"I'm just too busy right now. We're on the cusp of summer. That means weddings. Where there are weddings, there are bridal showers. And all of that is in addition to graduation parties. On top of which people still celebrate birthdays."

"You don't even need to check your schedule?" he asked.

This was awkward. Actually, she amended, she was awkward. She didn't know how to do this. She didn't want to do this. And, for Pete's sake, what part of no didn't he understand?

"Look, you said yourself that you're trying to simplify your life. You're going to be an empty-nester soon. I think this dating thing is a knee-jerk reaction to that."

"You're wrong. It's a knee-jerk reaction to wanting to see you socially."

Now what? Straightforward refusal, that's what. "I just can't. I'm sorry, Scott."

"I'm sorry, too." After an awkward moment, he turned and walked to the door, putting his hand on the knob. "Thanks for letting me barge in. I hope it wasn't too much trouble."

"Not at all. It was my idea."

"Yeah. I remember. Good night." Then he was gone.

Feeling like the slime that formed on rotten vegetables in the refrigerator, she stared at the spot where he'd been standing a second before. She was relieved that he'd finally accepted her no. But she couldn't help the tiniest bit of disappointment, too. Which was stupid since she didn't want to go out with him. She didn't have room in her life.

Shaking her head, she realized it had been a long time since she'd thought in terms of having a life. After losing David, it had really and truly felt as if a part of her had died, too. Coming back had been long and painful but she was getting there. The problem with having a life was the potential for complications.

There was no question she found Scott attractive. Everything about him appealed to her. He was a good man and a good father. It was impossible not to like him. But that was useless information. She was going to have a baby. Thanks to modern science, she didn't need a man and that was just fine with her.

Having her husband's baby wasn't the only vow Thea had made on David's deathbed. She'd also promised herself that she would never want or need a man again. And she'd just made sure there was no chance of that happening.

Chapter Seven

Scott walked into his younger brother's office at Matthews and Sons and slapped a folder down on the desk.

Mike Matthews glanced up from the spreadsheet on his computer screen. "Something wrong?"

Scott looked at his brother, working at the computer as if he didn't have a care in the world. And he probably didn't, because he'd never married and had kids. Not that Scott regretted his kids. He did, however, regret the woman he'd chosen to be their mother.

People had always said the two of them looked like twins. But that was where the resemblance stopped. Mike wore wire-rimmed glasses, compliments of being a computer geek. And his position as a desk jockey, instead of out in the field doing construction, meant that to stay fit he spent lots of time in the gym. Other than the fact that he envied his brother's simple lifestyle—no commitment, no way, no how—they were good friends. But he didn't really want to answer the question—was anything wrong?

"No," he finally said. "Why?"

Mike swiveled his desk chair and faced front. "Scuttlebutt has it that mortgage rates are expected to creep up. That could slow new home sales."

Scott shrugged. "Not in this area. Santa Clarita is booming and shows no signs of slowing down."

"I heard Josh McCardle is quitting. Isn't he your best crew foreman?"

"Yeah. Richmond West is really busy and offered him a better deal than we could. I told him to take it."

"He's been with the company for ten years. You taught him everything. Doesn't it tick you off that he went with a busy company—and our biggest competitor?"

Busy. That's what Thea had said. She was too busy to go out to dinner with him. She might just as well have said he was ugly and his mother dressed him funny. Too busy meant the same thing. Everyone had to eat. How could you be too busy to go out to dinner? It wasn't like he was asking her to sleep with him. He just wanted to take her out to a damn dinner.

Hell, who was he kidding? He wanted Thea any way he could get her. And if a romantic rendezvous afterwards at her place was in the cards, he wouldn't wimp out and throw in his hand.

"Scott?"

"Hmm?"

"You look like someone left your favorite drill out in the rain to rust. What's up with you?"

"Nothing."

"Something wrong with the girls? Did Kendra get turned down at UCLA?"

"No. The girls are fine."

His brother leaned back in his chair and linked his fingers over his abdomen. "Look, bro, you've been in a crap mood for a week now. I'm trying to be supportive, but I gotta tell you, playing twenty questions is getting real old. Either you tell me what's wrong or get out of my office. I don't much care which."

Scott released a long breath and stared out the window for several moments. "Okay. You win. Besides, I'm going to explode if I don't talk to someone about this."

"I'm here for you, Scott, you know that."

"I know you've had a lot of experience with women."

Mike's eyebrows shot up in surprise. "This is about a woman?"

The skeptical look on his brother's face didn't do anything to sweeten Scott's mood. "Don't look so shocked."

"Sorry. I can't help it. It's been a long time between women for you." He shrugged. "I just didn't think—"

"That I could have a problem with one?"

"Well, yeah." He grinned. "You made it clear that your personal life ran a distant third behind the girls and your job. It never occurred to me that you've been walking around in a black funk for a week and it was all about a woman."

"So it's breaking news?"

"I'm proud of you, bro."

"Don't be." Scott snorted. "She turned me down flat."

"Who is she?"

"Her name is Thea Bell and she owns a catering business here in town. I've hired her to take care of Ken's graduation party."

"And she's hot?"

"She's a very nice, very attractive woman," he answered. His tone must have held a warning because Mike lifted a hand as if to say she's all yours.

"She must be all that and more to get your attention."

"What does that mean?" Scott asked.

"Just that since your divorce, you haven't shown enough interest in any woman to walk around in a funk for a day, let alone a week."

Scott sat on the corner of the desk and blew out a long breath. "Here's the thing, Mike. She's different. She's not the type who talks much about her personal life."

"So ask her out and get to know her."

"I did. Like I said. She rejected me."

"What did she say?"

"That she was too busy."

Mike winced. "Ooh. That's bad."

"Even I know that. But it gets worse."

"How?"

"She knows Kendra is graduating from high school and going to college. She said that my asking her for a date was a knee-jerk reaction to the fact that I'll be an empty-nester."

"Ouch." Mike shook his head. "But you defended yourself, right? Set her straight?"

"I didn't think my ego could handle it. I got the feeling she was trying to let me down easy. It seemed to me if I pushed her, and she let me down any easier, I'd be a rust-colored stain on the carpet."

"Yeah. I can see how you'd get that impression."

Scott rubbed the back of his neck. "But here's the other thing, Mike. I really like her. And I know I'm not the sharpest tool in the shed where women are concerned, but I would bet my favorite hammer that she likes me, too."

"So?"

"So, I guess I could accept a *No* more gracefully if she just flat out said she's not interested."

"You want it up front and right between the eyes?" Mike asked.

"Yeah, I guess I do."

That was preferable to having children and spending years with a woman only to find out he didn't know her at all. After Kendra was born, he'd thought things were better than ever between him and his wife. So when she gave him her sweeping pronouncement that she wasn't happy being a wife and mother, it had come out of nowhere. And her timing couldn't have been worse. He'd been patting himself on the back for making it over the speed bumps in their marriage. Hell, he'd taken pride in the fact that they'd nipped their problems in the bud and were going to make it as a family. Then, to find out he'd been so wrong, he'd felt like the world's biggest chump.

"Maybe Thea's married," Mike suggested.

Scott shook his head. "She's a widow."

"Could be she's already got a boyfriend." Mike leaned forward and rested his forearms on his desk. "But if she does, wouldn't she just say so?"

Scott would be the first to admit he wasn't the best judge of character. But his gut was telling him that Thea was outspoken and direct. If she was personally involved with another guy she wouldn't hesitate to say so.

"Yeah. She would have been up front about dating someone else."

"So what's her deal?" Mike asked.

"Damned if I know."

And that was the hell of it. He didn't know. Not even what tragedy had taken her husband from her too soon. If he knew what was good for him, he would just drop the subject. Get through his daughter's party and walk away in one piece. Forget about Thea Bell. Why should he stick his neck out? Why put himself on the line again? He didn't much enjoy feeling like he'd been flattened by a speeding locomotive.

The thing was, he had a feeling Thea had been flattened even worse than he had. And he'd been telling the God's honest truth when he said he liked her. How long had it been since he'd met a woman he could say that about? He wasn't willing to blow it off without at least giving it another try.

He met his brother's gaze. "Mikey, I'm going to find out what her deal is if it's the last thing I do."

"That's the spirit. But, Scotty—"

"Yeah?"

"Don't ever call me Mikey again. If you do, I'm gonna have to hurt you."

Scott grinned. "You and what army?"

But he felt better than he had in a week. Because now he had a plan. Come hell or high water, he intended to find out personal information about Ms. Thea Bell.

"I'm grounded."

"But why?" Thea asked, settling herself on the sofa.

She'd arrived for her appointment with Scott at the agreed-upon time but he wasn't home from work yet. Kendra had let her in and invited her to sit in the family room. The first words out of her mouth were about her punishment.

"He's so unreasonable. I came in just a little after my curfew."

Thea remembered what Scott had told her about the rule. "I guess he figures if he gives an inch you'll take a mile."

"But it's not fair."

"He said you were working on something for school. Did you need more time."

Kendra shrugged. "It took a little longer than we thought."

"I don't get the impression your dad is completely unreasonable. Did you call and explain the situation?"

"With my dad that's a waste of time and cell phone minutes."

"So you didn't even try?"

The teen flopped back on the couch. "My battery was dead. I tried to explain, but he said being grounded will give me time to think about remembering to plug it in."

Scott *was* tough as nails, Thea thought. In the same situation, she'd have been tempted to relax the rules, as long as schoolwork was involved. But she could certainly see the wisdom of running a tight ship the way he did.

"But what about your friend's house? Is it a cave without phone service?" Thea's mouth curved up. "No, let me guess. Both of your hands were broken and you couldn't dial the phone. And all your friends had the same problem."

The girl grinned reluctantly. "No. Zoe's house has a working phone. But I forgot because…"

"What?" she asked, when the girl got a funny look on her face.

She didn't quite meet Thea's gaze. "Because we left."

"And? What aren't you telling me?"

"Zoe wanted to go to Java 'n Jazz where her boyfriend works. He was going to ask her to prom and we all got excited. I didn't think. And—"

"There's more?" Thea asked, surprised.

"Dad says Zoe doesn't have enough parental supervision and he's not happy about me hanging out with her."

The way things turned out, he was right to be concerned, Thea thought. But all she said was, "A rule is a rule."

"You sound just like him. He said the same thing. Followed by—and I quote—next time you won't forget." She heaved a big sigh.

Thea reached over and patted her arm. "I'd love to bash your father with you," she lied. "Except I agree with him."

"Traitor." But there was no heat or hostility in the word.

"Tell me honestly that if he relaxed the rule on this, you wouldn't push the envelope again under the same circumstances. Or next time you're out on a school night working on a project with your friends, tell me you won't remember this consequence and be home by curfew."

Kendra tucked a strand of long dark hair, the same shade as her father's, behind her ear. "Okay. You might have a point."

"I knew you were a reasonable young woman the first time I met you."

"Not so much," the girl said. "I plan to stay mad at my dad for a long time."

"You might consider one thing."

"What?"

"He's letting you have a catered graduation party *and* picking up the tab. And I'm not just saying that because I got the job."

Kendra's shoulders slumped as she shook her head. "I hate it when people are rational, logical and sensible."

"I can be annoying that way," Thea agreed.

The teen met her gaze. "So you think I should be nice to him?"

"I think you should accept your punishment gracefully and move on." She tapped her lip thoughtfully. "If you really want to freak him out, tell him you completely understand why he punished you, then thank him for caring so much."

Kendra grinned. "You're diabolical."

"It drove my parents crazy," she agreed. She opened the notebook on her lap. "Did you taste the dishes I left?"

The teen nodded. "I loved them all. Especially the lasagna and quesadilla. The Greek salad not so much. Egg rolls," she closed her eyes and heaved a huge sigh. "To die for."

"So do you want to do an international sort of menu?"

"Dad said you didn't mind if that's what I wanted."

Thea nodded. "It makes no difference to me. Like I told him, the client is always right."

"Then how come I got grounded?"

"Because you were wrong not to follow your father's rules." Thea looked at her. "You might want to consider law school after college. Way to twist the daylights out of an innocent remark."

"Thanks." Kendra grinned proudly. Then she asked, "Isn't it more expensive to mix up different foods?"

Thea shook her head. "It's all about the ingredients. If you wanted a recipe with shrimp, lobster or crab or something with expensive fixings, I'd have to pass on the cost to your father."

"What are the most expensive things you make?" the girl asked, a gleam in her eyes.

"Oh, no you don't. I'm not getting caught in the middle of World War III."

Thea heard the front door open and close and her heart skipped a beat. Scott was home. She'd been half relieved and half disappointed he wasn't there when she'd arrived. Although mostly she dreaded seeing him again after their awkward last meeting. If only he hadn't tried to make things personal. Under different circumstances, she would have been like a teenage girl at her first boy/girl party. But letting things between them become more than a simple business association was a recipe for disaster. And she'd had enough of that to last her a lifetime.

The teen grinned at her just before her father walked into the room. "Hi, Dad."

"Hey, sweetie." He looked surprised, as if he'd expected hostility. "Sorry I'm late, Thea."

"No, problem. It gave Kendra and I a chance to talk things over."

"What things?"

The teen stood and walked over to him. She kissed his cheek. "I just wanted to say thanks for grounding me. I deserved it, and I'm sorry I broke the rules."

He stared at his daughter as if she'd beamed down from the Starship Enterprise before his very eyes. "You are?"

"I'm going upstairs to do my homework."

"Okay," he said.

"See you later, Thea. Thanks for talking with me."

"Any time," she said.

Although she'd rather the teen stick around and not leave her alone with Scott. But after advising her to shake him up, she couldn't very well ruin this Kodak moment.

After his daughter disappeared upstairs, Scott slid her a shell-shocked look. "Do you want to explain that?"

"No."

"So there is an explanation?"

"I didn't say that."

"It was implied," he said.

"She's your daughter."

"Maybe." He glanced up at the ceiling, where his child had disappeared. "Or maybe my daughter was kidnapped by aliens who left a very cooperative, very scary clone in her place."

Thea laughed. "She's a good kid. Leave it at that."

"Okay." He set his briefcase on the floor by a wing chair. "I hope I didn't keep you waiting too long. I got hung up in a meeting with my brother Mike."

"No problem. It gave Kendra and I a chance to discuss what she wants for food. She decided to do an international smorgasbord. Lasagna, quesadillas, egg rolls. I recommend a big green salad and fresh fruit salad with that."

"So are we talking a second mortgage on my house to cover it?" he teased.

"Actually, I explained to her that the ingredients of a recipe determine the cost. She wanted to know what my most expensive main dishes are."

"And?" he said cringing.

"You walked in and she became teen angel." Thea

shrugged. "Actually she approved all of your choices. Apparently you have similar taste."

When he smiled, she felt instant heat roll through her followed by a melting sensation that made her thighs quiver. Why did this have to happen to her now? Everything in her life was going perfectly. Her business was better than ever. Financially she was secure. She had a baby on the way that would fulfill a deeply personal promise as well as a powerful maternal yearning. And now she was attracted to *this* man.

Since she couldn't deny it any longer, she would simply have to deal with it. She stood. "Now all you have to do is give me the number of people and I can work up the figures for you."

"Ken and I will talk that over. Now that we're talking, period. I have a feeling that change in our communication is thanks to you," he added.

"Sooner or later it would have blown over. Talking just made the process go faster." It was nothing more than the truth because he'd done a wonderful job with his children. He was a terrific father. And that thought shook her, convincing her it was time to get back on task before she had to examine her feelings too closely. "When you have a guest list, I'll know how many tables to reserve."

He folded his arms over his chest, and the impossibly masculine pose snagged her feminine attention in spite of her best intentions. She noticed that whole heat thing again with the fireball effect in the pit of her belly. Every nerve ending in her body zapped a hormone, which she had in spades at the moment. The chain reaction let her know how aware she was of this man.

"What about setting up outside?" he asked.

She glanced out the slider into the backyard. "Good

idea. The pool will make a wonderful focal point. And you have lots of room, so table arrangements shouldn't be a problem."

"Unless Kendra wants to invite the equivalent of a third world country."

"Yes." She inched toward the exit. "But that's for the two of you to work out."

His gaze narrowed. "What's your rush? Do you have another appointment?"

"No, I—"

Whenever she was around Scott Matthews, she felt like a pacemaker too close to microwaves. All her brain functions went haywire. He'd just given her an out. All she'd needed to say was that she had to be somewhere. It wasn't even a lie. She did have to be somewhere— anywhere but spitting distance from this man would do.

"I have to get going," she said, hoping to salvage the situation. "I need to—

The doorbell rang and he held up a hand. "That's our pizza. Hold that thought."

She didn't want to hold anything. She just wanted to go and distract herself from thoughts of Scott Matthews. After she'd refused to go out with him, she'd feared a cool and distant working relationship. He was anything but. Charming was the word that came to mind. Talk about diabolical. But his lack of a grudge wasn't something she could let herself get excited about.

It had been a long time since she'd felt anything but emptiness. But her baby and meeting Scott had changed that. She couldn't stop the feeling. It was exciting to be attracted to a good-looking man. But fate had a twisted sense of humor because he was the wrong man.

He walked back into the kitchen with a large flat box

and a bag on top of it. "Dinner is served." His expression turned wry. "I'm sure it's not as good as what you could make."

"I love pizza."

"Stay and have some with us."

She'd done it again. If this kept up, she'd have to find a good recipe for foot-in-mouth. "I don't want to intrude."

"It's not intruding if I invite you. Besides, anyone who can get my daughter to thank me for punishing her is someone I want to know better."

"It's only because I'm not an authority figure."

Scott studied her. "How did you get to know so much about teenagers? Did you study teen psychology in school?"

"I was a business major, actually." Wow, did that pizza smell good.

"Did you go to college in California?"

"UC Santa Barbara."

"Did you grow up here?" He flipped back the square top of the box and the mouth-watering smell permeated the room. "Do you have family in the area? Brothers and sisters?" He handed her a paper plate with a triangle of pizza on it.

She took it and after taking a bite and chewing, she said, "My parents live in Northridge. I have a brother in San Diego and a sister in Marina Del Rey."

"A boyfriend?" He took a bite of his own pizza and met her gaze.

She put her plate down. "If I did have one, I would have said so the last time we were together." When he'd asked her out, but she didn't want to say that. Wasn't he the nosy one. It was time to put the brakes on that. "Thanks for the pizza, Scott. But I really have to go."

"Why? You don't have an appointment."

"That doesn't mean I don't have things to do."

"What is it with you and questions?"

"An exchange of personal information is a technique for bonding. Since we have nothing more than a short-term business contract that would be a waste of time."

"We can't be friends?"

"This can be a friendly *working* relationship," she said, emphasizing the key word.

Scott put down his paper plate and frowned. "I don't get you."

It's really not that complicated, she thought. One tidbit of info would lead to another and another. It could take them to a place she would rather not go.

"I'm sorry. But you know better than anyone that there are rules. Your daughter can't stay out past ten on a school night. I make it a point not to get too close to my clients." She shrugged. "I've found it's better that way."

"For who?"

"Everyone." She picked up her things. "Call me when you and Kendra have the guest list together."

Thea walked out the front door before he could say anything more. When she was inside her car, she had the most absurd desire to burst into tears. It was really stupid since she was the one who had done the walking out. She felt so bad curbing her normally friendly nature, but Scott seemed determined not to let it go. She was a couple weeks shy of completing her first trimester and discussing the baby until then was out of the question.

But how she wanted to. The temptation to laugh and talk with him about it was almost too much to resist. He'd been a father twice over and knew what to expect. Just being in the same room with him made her feel—

What? More than simple attraction, that was a given. He was strong and conscientious, the kind of man who took care of his own. She'd missed sharing the load with someone. And she was tired of being alone.

She wouldn't be for very much longer. Soon she'd have her baby. And she'd be raising it alone. It wasn't as if she hadn't known before the IVF, so she had no right to whine. But she was acutely aware of coming back to life because Scott made her ache for what she couldn't have.

If she *were* a whiner, that was prime complaint criteria.

Chapter Eight

Thea closed the book she'd just finished and set it on the end table beside her. She wondered if she'd have time to read after the baby was born. Pressing her palms against her abdomen, she longed for the six and a half months to pass quickly. If it weren't for the weariness and nausea that were tangible signs of her pregnancy, she would have her doubts about a baby growing inside her.

It seemed like forever until she would be able hold it in her arms. She prayed the child she carried would be healthy and perfect.

A knock on her door startled her and she looked at her watch. "Eight-thirty? I'm not expecting anyone."

At the door, she stood on tiptoe to see through the peephole as she called out, "Who is it?"

"Kendra Matthews."

Several things went through her mind at once when she recognized the teen. It was too late for a strictly social visit. Scott must have shared with his daughter the location of the condo he intended to buy. But why would she come here? Something was wrong and Thea wasn't sure she wanted to get involved. Shaking her head, she realized there was no choice. She hadn't been able to ignore this girl from the first time she'd met her.

Thea sighed as she turned the dead bolt and opened the door. "Hi, kiddo. Come in."

"Hi, Thea." The girl walked inside and stood in the entryway twisting her fingers together. "I'm sorry to bother you."

"You didn't. In fact your timing is perfect. I just finished my book." She frowned as she recognized the intensely tragic expression on the girl's face. "What's wrong?"

"I had a fight with my dad."

"I'm sorry." Thea was no expert on teenage behavior, but it seemed weird for Kendra to show up here instead of going to someone her own age.

"Can I talk to you?"

"Of course. But I'm surprised you didn't go to one of your friends."

"They're gone. Zoe invited all of us to go to the Colorado River with her and her mom and stepdad."

"Your dad wouldn't let you go," Thea guessed.

She nodded miserably. "He says she's not a good influence after what happened to get me grounded. She's a new friend, and he's never met her parents. So he just put his foot down and said no. He wouldn't even listen to me or give her another chance. I got so frustrated, I just left."

"He doesn't know where you are?"

She shook her head. "I turned off my cell phone."

Thea wanted to insist the girl call her father. If she

were in Scott's shoes and her child had stormed out of the house, she would be frantic. But she had a feeling if she insisted, the teen might take off again. Then she would be behind the wheel of a car with her emotions all over the map. Not a safe situation.

"Come in and sit down," she invited. "Can I get you a soda? Something to eat? Have you had dinner?"

"I'm not hungry." She sat on the sofa and set her keys on the coffee table.

Thea understood Scott's protectiveness. Her baby wasn't even born yet and she was bending over backwards to make sure this child would have a full-term pregnancy and safe delivery into this world. She could only imagine how her instincts to safeguard this child would escalate when she held him for the first time and watched him grow.

Scott had nurtured his daughter for eighteen years. Even when his decisions were met with hostility and rebellion, he kept his head and tried the best he knew how to do the right thing. She couldn't fault him.

"You know your dad doesn't take pleasure in telling you no."

"He's so unreasonable."

"Translation—he wouldn't let you do what you wanted."

The teen met her gaze and her eyes widened in surprise. "You're taking his side?"

Thea refused to be put on the defensive. "Why did you come here Kendra?"

She lifted one shoulder. "To talk, I guess."

"And I'm happy to do that," Thea said, sitting beside her. "But part of talking is listening. And I'm not the kind of person who will say what you want to hear. I'll tell you what I think."

"You think my dad is right? That Zoe is a bad person?"

"I have no opinion on your friend. I've never met her. And I'm not convinced your dad thinks that, either."

"He doesn't trust my judgment."

"Think about it from his point of view. All he knows is that you went to her house to study and then you broke the rules."

"His rules are lame." She slouched against the back of the sofa.

"Maybe. But as long as you live under his roof and he's paying the bills, he's entitled to set any parameters he thinks best."

"So you think I should go away to college, too."

Thea stared at this woman/child who'd just leaped from the specific to the general. "It doesn't matter what I think and that's not what we were talking about. Here's the thing—even if you go away to college, your dad will still be paying the bills. He's still going to have some input in your life. Not as much input, and not on a day-to-day basis. The only way to have things your own way is to be independent. And the only way I can see for you to do that is to suck it up and get the best possible education so you can support yourself and not rely on your father."

The girl's eyes grew wide. Obviously she hadn't expected to hear she needed to snap out of it. Finally, one corner of her mouth turned up. "It will take forever to get through college."

"'The journey of a thousand miles starts with a single step,'" Thea quoted. "Besides, I bet when you were a freshman in high school you thought you'd never graduate. Yet here you are."

"Yeah. It seems like a long time ago. How did you know?"

"Because I remember. It felt like I'd be in high school forever. Suddenly I was a senior and saying goodbye to my friends. It was a scary, exciting, traumatic time."

"I know what you mean," she said, sitting up straight. "I get so weird sometimes—"

A knock on the door interrupted her. "I wonder who that could be," Thea said. She stood and walked over, too tired to strain and see who was there. "Who is it?"

"Scott Matthews."

At the sound of his voice, Thea felt the shivery sensation he always generated flutter through her. The good news was it chased her weariness away. The bad news: as much as she knew it wasn't smart to be in the same room with him, she just couldn't turn him away.

"I'm going to let him in." She glanced over her shoulder. When the girl nodded, Thea put her hand on the knob and opened the door.

"I saw Kendra's car," he said, before she could greet him.

The expression on his face was grim, ragged, intense. When he looked past her and saw his daughter, relief was stark on his features even before he released a long breath. He walked inside. "Hi," he said to her.

She stood up. "How did you know I was here?"

"When you didn't answer your cell, I decided to drive around and see if I could spot your car. I knew all your friends were gone, so I came by here on a hunch. Process of elimination." He shrugged. "I was worried about you, Ken."

"I'm sorry, Dad. I just needed some space. I get so frustrated." She twisted her fingers together.

He nodded. "Me, too. Welcome to my world."

"Thea made me look at things from your point of view."

"Good. But I think we've imposed on Thea long enough."

When he glanced at her, Thea couldn't tell what he was thinking. But she was thinking how good it was to see him.

Kendra picked up her keys from the coffee table, then met Thea's gaze. "Thanks for making me listen."

"Any time."

The teen looked at her father. "I'll see you at home."

"Okay," he said. When she was gone, he finally looked at Thea. "I'm sorry she bothered you. But I have to ask what you said to her."

"I simply tried to give her a different perspective on the situation."

"So you didn't take her side?"

She put her hand on her hip. "What is it with you people? You're so hung up on taking sides. She accused me of taking yours. And you thought I'd take hers."

He grinned. "So you didn't hang me out to dry. I like that in a friend."

"Are we? Friends, I mean?" What had made her ask that? She was the one bending over backward to keep it professional. A *friendly* working relationship, she'd said.

"You tell me." He ran his fingers through his hair. "I've always made it a point to get friendly with the people surrounding my children. Kendra trusts you. You obviously have some influence over her. A positive one," he said, glancing at the door where his daughter had just left. "That is not the same girl who screamed that I was ruining her life just before she slammed out of the house a little while ago. And whatever you said to her is responsible for the attitude adjustment."

"I'm glad I could help."

"Me, too." He folded his arms over his chest. "But to answer your question. Are we friends? I don't know. But I'd like to be. Except I was taught that it's a two-way street. With you, I feel like a jaywalker every time I try."

"It's not you, Scott. It's me."

Suddenly he walked over to the end table and picked up an eight-by-ten picture frame sitting there and looked at it. "Is this your husband?"

"David," she said, as the familiar feeling of sadness washed through her.

"What happened to him?" When she hesitated, he said, "I wasn't aware that your life was subject to government security clearance. Besides the fact that in my world friends share things, I figure it's my job to know the people who influence my daughter. But that's just me. I'll try to make sure she doesn't bother you any more." He turned to leave.

"Wait!"

She didn't want him to leave like that. Somehow he'd become more than just a client. And she hadn't meant to hurt him.

"It's not just you," she said with a sigh. "I don't blurt out my personal information to just anyone. And I have my reasons." When one of his eyebrows lifted, she shook her head. "I don't expect you to understand. But I've learned to be cautious about sharing details."

"What about sharing the burden? When you mentioned David, you looked sad. What happened to him, Thea?" he asked, setting the picture back on the end table.

Looking at the familiar and beloved face, she realized that without a photo she had trouble remembering her husband's features. She couldn't figure out when that had happened.

"He died of cancer."

"I'm sorry," he automatically said.

"Me, too. He was way too young and it stinks."

"I'm sorry," he said again.

"It's all right. I'm over it."

"Yeah. I could tell by the 'it stinks' part. And the fact that you look like you're going to cry."

"Just hormones." Which was the truth.

During the in vitro process, she'd been pumped full of them to get her body ready to accept and nurture the implanted embryos. Now that she was pregnant, the hormones were still creating havoc in her body. But that didn't always explain why her eyes filled with tears. It was simply the reason she couldn't stop crying once she'd started.

Gently, Scott nudged her chin up with his knuckle and forced her to meet his gaze. "Thea, you don't have to do it alone. I'm here to listen."

When he curved his fingers around her upper arms, she allowed him to pull her against him. She rested her cheek on his chest, savoring the strong and steady beat of his heart. It had been so long since she'd leaned on anyone. God help her, it felt so good to be held. The circle of Scott's arms was a place she wished she could stay forever. Which was exactly why she pulled back.

When she did, she saw the hungry expression in his eyes. Part of her brain registered the fact that she recognized it. With the other part, she acknowledged her own corresponding sensual awareness that had been dormant for a long time.

It was the only explanation for her sigh of satisfaction when Scott eased her closer, then lowered his head to touch his mouth to hers. Instantly, liquid warmth trickled through her. He tunneled his fingers into her hair and lightly applied pressure to make the meeting of their mouths firmer.

Tenderly he moved his lips over hers, touching the corner of her mouth, the curve of her cheek, her nose and eyelids. The sweetness of it created an ache inside her. Moist heat settled between her quivering thighs and almost of their own will, her arms found their way around his neck. Then he slanted his mouth across hers again as his arm came around her waist, settling her against the solid, muscled length of him.

Her breath caught at the incredibly wonderful sensation of a man's hard body pressed to her feminine curves. The thought was like tossing a lighted match to bone-dry twigs. The resulting inferno threatened to consume her and she couldn't find the will to care.

Scott held her tightly to him and heaved a ragged sigh. She heard it at the same time his breath fanned her face and cranked up her need. When he pulled back a little, everything inside her cried out against ending the embrace.

"I didn't mean to do that," he said, resting his forehead to hers. "I'm a little out of practice."

"You couldn't prove it by me," she whispered.

As soon as the words left her mouth, she wanted them back in the worst way. She'd barely acknowledged her feelings of friendship for this man and now was revealing how much she'd enjoyed his kiss—so much, she'd have willingly followed him anywhere.

That thought scared Thea to the core of her being.

Carved on the wall of the church where she'd had her husband's funeral were the words "Grief is the price we pay for loving." In the weeks and months following, she'd decided the price was too high.

Only her promise to have this child had brought her through and given her the will to go on. But she wanted no part of loving a man ever again.

She stepped away from Scott. "Kendra will be waiting for you." She let out a long breath and stuffed her shaking hands into her pockets.

"Yeah." He ran a hand through his hair and she noticed he was shaking, too. The realization gave her no satisfaction. "I'll call you."

"Okay. There are still party details to work out."

She knew she was ducking behind her professional facade, but she had nowhere else to hide. Fortunately, he didn't comment. He simply nodded, then left her alone.

She locked the dead bolt and leaned back against the door, completely appalled at her behavior. She wished she could blame him. Heck, she wished she could dislike him.

But she couldn't do either. She could only put the brakes on her emotions to keep from liking him any more than she already did.

Thea hummed a popular tune as she walked into the office and set down her purse and briefcase. "Isn't it a beautiful day?"

"Good news?" Connie asked. She was sitting at her desk in the front office.

"The best."

Thea didn't need a mirror to see that she was beaming. She could feel it. Along with the pregnancy glow she'd heard so much about. It had to be evident to everyone who saw her. Flush, blush, shine, whatever.

She could practically feel it radiating from her and bouncing off stationary objects.

"So what did the doctor say?" her friend prompted impatiently.

"She said everything is progressing normally."

Connie sniffed. "I could have told you that."

"Yes, but she had the ultrasound results to prove it." She put a hand on her abdomen. "Seriously, Con, I'm so relieved. She said there's no reason to expect anything out of the ordinary, even though this baby was conceived through in vitro fertilization."

"So you're just like every other hormone-riddled woman who's going to give birth in six months?"

Thea nodded enthusiastically. "The method of conception doesn't make me any more vulnerable to miscarriage or any other pregnancy trauma than a woman who gets pregnant the old-fashioned way."

Speaking of sex, Thea flashed back to the memory of Scott kissing her. She couldn't help wondering if her baby was the only thing responsible for her glow.

"Speaking of sex," Connie began.

They'd been friends too long. It was as if they could read each other's mind.

Thea knew what was coming and didn't want to go there. "We weren't talking about sex. I was referring to the miracle of modern science that made this baby possible."

"No, you were referring to the time-honored tradition of the horizontal hokey-pokey that sometimes results in pregnancy if the sperm is not deflected from its intended target."

"No. I was referring to the fact that simply because my baby was helped along in its existence, that doesn't mean I can't enjoy a routine, worry-free pregnancy.

Using common sense, there's no reason I have to limit my normal activities."

"So you're cleared for sex," Connie clarified wryly.

"Sex might be listed under normal for most pregnant women, but not for me. And it hasn't been for over two years."

"Even more reason to be open to the possibilities."

Thea narrowed her gaze. "What does that mean?"

Connie stood and crossed her arms over her chest as she leaned back against her own desk. The expression on her face said what she had on her mind wasn't the usual attitude-laced, bracing, rah-rah pep talk. She had something serious to say.

"David died, Thea, not you."

"I'm aware of that."

"He was your husband and you loved him. He was my friend and I loved him. I introduced the two of you in college. I wish I could say I did it because I thought he was perfect for you, but that would be a lie. I simply got tired of you whining that you never met any nice guys."

"I didn't whine."

Connie's grin was fleeting. "So not the point. Here's the thing, Thea. David loved you very much and would want you to get every last drop of fun and fulfillment out of life."

"And that's what I'm doing," she defended. "I'm going to have a child."

"David's child."

"Yes. I promised him."

"Are you sure it's not just another barrier to keep anyone from getting close to you again?"

A knot formed inside her and Thea fought down the annoyance. "How can you say that? You knew David almost as well as I did. You know how much he wanted children. We wanted to create a child who would inherit the best of our combined DNA. His brains, my—"

"Stubbornness?"

"That's not what I was going to say."

Connie sighed. "You met a terrific guy—"

"I meet lots of guys."

"Okay, you want to split hairs, I can get specific. Scott Matthews."

Thea's heart pounded merely at the mention of his name. "What about him?"

"He's better looking than the average bear. He's pretty well-off financially. He seems like a great guy and his daughter likes you."

"And what's your point?" As if she didn't know.

"He's interested in you."

"Get real," Thea scoffed, hoping to pull off disinterest so her friend would drop the subject.

"I will if you will." Connie braced her hands on the desk, then slid her fanny on top and let her legs dangle. "He's interested. And I think you are, too."

"Oh, for Pete's sake."

"No, for your sake. And your baby's. That child is important. No one understands that better than me. But you're poising yourself to make it the center of your universe and that's just not normal."

"I'm not doing that," she protested.

"You are. You're shutting down feelings with real potential."

"How do you know this?"

"Because I'm your best friend." When she started to protest, Connie held up her hand. "Can you honestly tell me that Scott Matthews hasn't made your inner woman sit up and do the happy dance?"

Thea shifted uncomfortably as she sighed and looked away.

"What?" Connie demanded. "I know you. What happened? Tell me everything. I can't believe you've been withholding details."

Thea finally met her gaze. "I could have told you my inner woman was comatose. And it would have been true before—"

"What?"

"Before Scott kissed me."

"Hot damn and hallelujah," Connie cheered.

"I don't know what you're so excited about. It didn't mean anything."

"Uh-oh." Her friend's gaze narrowed. "Please tell me you're not going to pooh-pooh it."

"Why not?"

"It's just wrong to spit in fate's eye like that."

"What are you talking about?" Thea asked. But the question was simply a stall, because she knew what was coming.

"There must be some kind of cosmic rule against turning your back on possibilities. For throwing away the opportunity for happiness."

"It's not happiness I object to," Thea said. "But the emptiness and pain that happen when it's taken away."

"So you *are* turning your back," Connie said in her aha-I-knew-it tone of voice.

"I'm being realistic. Scott Matthews is everything you said. And in case there's any doubt, I did, in fact, notice he's not hard on the eyes."

"I hear a but."

"But he's nearly finished raising his children."

"Look at it this way. He brings experience to the table."

"That's just it. He doesn't want to sit at the table. He wants footloose and fancy-free. But I'll be tied down for the next eighteen years."

Longer, really. She could see that because of what Scott was dealing with. The hands-on responsibility would change, but it would always be there. Because the love would always be there.

"You're having a child. It's not one of those prisoner ankle surveillance things," the other woman said. "You can still have a personal life with all the lows, highs and in betweens. You're entitled to the joys of living. Including sex."

Thea was living. She knew that because of the way her body had come alive and burned at the feel of Scott's mouth on her own. What scared her the most was that she would have slept with him. She wasn't sure how or why she'd gotten to that point, but she had.

And it would have been wrong. For both of them. For so many reasons.

She looked at her friend. "I know I have a life to live. Now I have this life inside me. This baby is the most important thing to me. I don't need the distraction of interpersonal relationships."

"Translation, you're running away."

"No. I'm running to. I'm looking forward to being a mother."

"What about a father?"

"That's out of my hands."

"No—"

"Stop, Con. I can't go there."

Connie emitted a huge sigh that meant defeat and Thea was grateful. She didn't want to argue. Her life was moving forward according to plan. And Scott Matthews was not now nor could he ever be a part of that plan.

After two miscarriages, this baby—her baby—had finally made it safely through the first trimester. With the baby growing inside her she'd kept her promise. She couldn't hope for more happiness than that.

She was afraid to.

Chapter Nine

Thea sat down at Scott's kitchen table and tried to forget that the last time she'd seen him he'd kissed the daylights out of her. It was time to pull herself together. Only a difficult, persnickety client got as much attention as she'd given him. And he was neither difficult nor persnickety. Which meant she'd subconsciously wanted to be with him. That had to stop. Firm decisions needed to be made so she could keep her distance.

"Okay. It's crunch time," she told him. And she didn't mean crunched up against that hard, strong body. So much for getting a grip.

"Are we really short on time?" he asked.

She shrugged sheepishly. "We're doing okay. I just like saying that."

"Ah, the dramatic type," he said with a quick grin. "I'll remember that. Before we get started, would you like a drink?"

"No, thanks."

"I've got coffee made."

She shook her head. "I'm off caffeine."

"Doctor's orders?" He glanced at her over his shoulder as he pulled a mug from the cupboard above the coffeemaker.

"Why would you think that?"

"No reason. You just seem nervous."

Not because of caffeine, she thought. Because of him. Because of that kiss.

"It's just a busy time of year for the business. I'm being pulled in a lot of different directions right now."

One of them was her attraction to Scott, a direction she refused to go. She'd been there, done that, and didn't want to participate ever again. It was exciting at first, but the potential for pain was too great. Best to just do this job and that would be that.

He set his mug on the kitchen table and sat down at a right angle to her. "Okay. Then we'll nail down this menu for Kendra's party so you can relax."

Like that was going to happen with him sitting a foot away from her. "Okay," she said, glancing at her notes. "We've got international delight here. And Kendra liked everything but the Greek salad. I had an idea how we could pull it off and still do justice to the food."

"I'm all ears."

If only that were true, she thought wishing he had Dumbo ears. If only he had a flaw to detract from his overwhelming appeal. Then her heart would idle in neutral instead of racing like a runaway locomotive.

She cleared her throat. "I was thinking we could serve the quesadillas and egg rolls as appetizers, then bring out the lasagna and garlic bread. I'll do an antipasto salad with a light Italian dressing. And the previously agreed-on fresh fruit salad."

Sipping his coffee, he nodded slightly. "Sounds good."

She lifted one eyebrow. Right. Neither difficult nor persnickety. "You're awfully accommodating. Why is that?"

"You'd rather I was a pain in the caboose?" He smiled. "I hired a catering professional. It wouldn't be especially bright to ignore her advice."

"I suppose not. What about dessert?"

"I'm always in favor of it," he agreed.

"I was thinking about a cake iced and decorated with her school colors. What are they, by the way?"

"Red and black."

"Yikes."

"Problem?"

"Challenge." She tapped her lip thoughtfully. "I have a recipe for a red velvet cake garnished with coconut. I'll put Connie to work on a creative angle to work in the black."

"Something that won't be too gross?"

"Guaranteed. Trust me."

He winced. "People always say that when it's the last thing you should do."

"I wouldn't steer you wrong." She made some notes, then met his gaze. Her heart stuttered at the intensity there as he studied her. "Shouldn't we run this by Kendra?"

"She's not here."

"I thought she was grounded. Did she have a get-out-of-jail-free card?"

"She had freshman orientation at UCLA. College always trumps consequences. It's a two-day overnighter."

"Wow. That's a major breakthrough for her. You must be happy."

At least one of them was. Now that she knew they

were alone, she was anything but thrilled. It was her cue to finish up and get the heck out of Dodge. She wasn't far off the mark when she'd said it was crunch time. Because she wanted so badly to kiss him again. She'd replayed the last one over and over in her mind and each time she was left with a yearning to feel his lips against hers one more time. With hormones spiking the way they were, she couldn't be held responsible for her actions.

"I have mixed emotions about her college weekend," he admitted. "And I understand I have you to thank for this."

"Should I be afraid?" she asked, leaning away from him.

He laughed. "No. She said she talked to you and you challenged her—pointed out that she had nothing to lose by gathering information."

"I did," she said nodding. "But I don't understand your reaction."

"That's because you don't have kids." He sighed. "As graduation gets closer, the local junior college looks more appealing because she could live at home. Considering recent bad choices on her part, that wouldn't be a bad thing. On the other hand, I'm glad she's at least exploring her options. Thinking about spreading her wings. But that's a scary thought, too."

Thea empathized with him, and, at the same time, she admired his parenting skills. He stepped in when necessary and stood back with bated breath the rest of the time. She thought about the baby she was carrying and what she would have to deal with when her child was a teenager. She'd be alone like Scott and hoped she handled it even half as well.

But that was personal and she was here on business.

"So she gave you full discretionary powers," she said to get them back on track.

"Yup. I get to pick whatever I want."

Thea met his gaze and her pulse skipped at the dark intensity there. He looked as if he'd like to pick *her*.

She stood suddenly. "Okay. I think we're finished with this part."

"We are?" He stood, too.

"You said, and I quote, 'Sounds good.' That's good enough for me. Now all I need from you is a maximum number of guests attending the party and I can firm up a price."

Scott put a hand on her arm. "Don't go, Thea."

"But I have stuff—"

"To do," he finished. "So do I, but that's not what this is about."

"No?" she said in a small voice.

He shook his head. "Caffeine isn't making you nervous. It was that kiss." She opened her mouth and he silenced her with a finger on her lips. "I think you liked it just as much as I did."

He'd liked it, too? Warmth spread through her until she threw cold water on it. One of them had to be realistic.

"It's not that simple, Scott."

"It can be." His expression sobered as he studied her. "Is this about your husband?"

"That's part of it."

"It's been two years, Thea. You're allowed to have a life." He took her hands in his and squeezed reassuringly. "You shouldn't feel guilty that you didn't die, too. There's not a doubt in my mind that if you could do anything to bring him back, you'd do it in a heartbeat."

She simply nodded when words stuck in her throat.

"Thea, I can't imagine you loving any man who wouldn't want you to move forward and be happy."

"It's not just that, Scott. There's more. I have to tell you—"

"Me first," he interrupted, then took her face in his hands and lowered his mouth to hers.

The tender touch set off a firestorm inside her and instantaneously passion ignited. Thea felt a hunger that had nothing to do with food and everything to do with her craving for a man's touch, the feel of his lips on hers, the taste of him, the longing to be in his arms.

She pressed as close to him as she could get, reveling in the feel of her softness against his rock-solid body. He groaned and tightened his hold on her. When he traced the seam of her lips, she opened to him. Heat billowed through her as his tongue invaded her mouth, the motivation imitating the act of lovemaking.

She heard a moan and it took her several moments to realize that wanton sound had come from her. Was it reckless? Maybe. Probably. But she couldn't find the will to care. The pleasure was vaguely familiar from another lifetime. Familiar, but so very different and new. Hot. Intense. Frantic.

Yet, she knew where she was going, what she was doing. And she could no more stop herself from experiencing the sensations of happiness in Scott's arms than she could flap her arms and fly to the moon.

This was sex. The affirmation of life. And the physical expression of her femininity. It was reassurance that she was a woman. She was alive and this man was attracted to her. That realization was more intoxicating than any alcohol.

A frightening excitement exploded through her body, unlike anything she'd ever experienced before. It went beyond pleasure and became simply a demanding need. One she couldn't deny.

Scott lifted his mouth from hers. "Thea," he said, his breath ragged. "I want you. If that's not okay, you need to tell me now."

She studied the sincerity on his face and realized she didn't have the words to express the depth of what she was feeling. "I want you, too," she simply said.

He shut his eyes for a moment and let out a long breath. "Thank God." Then he looked at her, his expression wary. "But I think it only fair to warn you I haven't done this in a pretty long time."

His admission only endeared him to her more. If he'd been arrogant and condescending, resisting him would be a piece of cake. But he was sweet, sexy and so very masculine. She was a goner.

"Me, either," she said. "We can muddle our way through together."

"I like the sound of that." His grin made her weak in the knees.

As if he'd read her mind, he scooped her into his arms. She squealed with surprise as she encircled his neck with her arms. "Scott, put me down. You'll hurt yourself."

"Way to make me feel manly," he teased. "You hardly weigh anything."

He headed for the stairs and easily carried her up to his bedroom. If she wasn't already a sure thing, she would be after this. The sheer romance of the gesture melted her insides like a Fudgsicle left in the sun.

Beside his bed, he removed his arm from behind her knees and let her body slide down the front of his. She felt the bulge in the front of his pants and reveled in the knowledge that he wanted her as much as she wanted him.

He took her face in his hands and kissed her thoroughly, nibbling his way across her cheek and over her jaw to the indentation beneath her ear. When he touched his tongue to the oh-my-God spot, her breath caught.

He slid his fingers up under her sweater and settled his palms on the bare flesh at her waist. The warmth of his palms felt too good and she realized how much she'd missed a man's touch. Did he miss being touched by a woman?

She slid his T-shirt from the waistband of his jeans and imitated his actions. When she settled her hands on his chest, he sucked in a breath. The sound of his approval was sustenance to her soul.

He looked at her, his expression tight and strained from passion and need. "Don't you think we have too many clothes on?"

"Yes," she said breathlessly.

In a frenzy of activity they pulled off shirts and pants and everything in between and stood there naked, simply looking their fill of each other. And suddenly the perfection of his body was too much for her. Thea knew if she didn't explore the muscular perfection with her hands, she would shrivel up and blow away.

She settled her palms on his chest again, loving the tingle from the dusting of hair. Sliding over the contours of his muscles, she felt his ribs and the firmness of his abdomen. Again he sucked in his breath and she knew where to touch to get his attention.

He lowered his head and kissed her. The assault of sensations made her dizzy: the firmness of his mouth; the taste of coffee; the startling, stimulating intimacy of his tongue stroking hers. She'd shut out memories of the warm smoothness of a man's skin, the spicy scent of his aftershave, the safety of his arms around her.

Suddenly her tender breasts were pressed against the unyielding wall of his chest. Her nipples tightened and throbbed in a way that made her revel in her femininity.

When he pulled back slightly, the intensity of his gaze burned her like twin blue flames. He half turned and yanked the bedcovers back. Then he scooped her up again, settled her in the center of his big bed and came down beside her.

His passion-filled gaze locked with hers. "I'm safe."

Desire made her brain misfire, but she got his drift. The only response she could manage was, "Me, too."

He nodded and settled his lips on hers. As he took her breast in his palm, she was swept away on a tide of emotion, excitement, anticipation. Need built within her as he rubbed her nipple between his fingers. He swallowed her moan of pleasure, then slid his hand down her abdomen and cupped her most feminine place in his palm.

Her already ragged breathing stuttered at the intimate, exquisite contact and liquid heat pooled there, getting her body ready for him. Then he slipped a finger inside her and she welcomed the intimacy. He explored the folds of her femininity and found the small nub encompassing all the nerve endings of her pleasure.

He stroked and rubbed until she was mindless with want. Tension built inside her and begged for release. Without warning, the pressure stretched and tore and exploded. She shattered into a million brilliant points of light, and her breath caught in her throat. Cares and worries and stress drained away and she felt boneless, like a rag doll.

Until he touched his tongue to that sensational spot by her ear. Just like that, her senses came to life. When he settled himself between her legs and nudged her knees apart, she gloried in the closeness. Then he slowly eased his way into her feminine passage. Her body was unaccustomed to this sort of intrusion and the care he took showed that he was aware. His tender sensitivity brought tears to her eyes.

He moved slowly at first, giving her time to become accustomed to him. When she arched her hips and accommodated his rhythm, he increased the pace, stroking in and out. His movements grew faster and more intense until he thrust one last time. His body went still as he groaned out his release and satisfaction.

Thea held him in her arms until his shudders stopped and he finally rolled away. She turned her head on the pillow and opened one eye. She saw that Scott was smiling.

"What's so funny?" she asked.

"Not a doggone thing. That was pretty sensational."

"It was amazing," she agreed, returning his smile.

He rolled to his side, then reached over and brushed her hair from her cheek. "I'm glad," he said sincerely.

"Me, too. I'd say we muddled through pretty well. You, sir, were way too modest about your muddling skills."

"As were you." He slid his arm around her and nestled her to his side. "If you're game, we can muddle again in a little while."

"I'll be a muddler if you will."

"Lady, I'll muddle with you any time, anywhere. Just say the word."

"Muddle," she said with a sigh.

For just this one night, she thought. Surely no one could begrudge her a single night of sweetness and light after so much darkness.

* * *

Scott felt something soft and warm move beside him. Then he got a jab in the chest and opened one eye. He smiled when he saw Thea with her shiny, silky brown hair spread across the pillow beside his. He opened his other eye to see her better.

He felt the need to touch her, make sure she was real. Gently, he smoothed a strand of hair from the corner of her mouth. Heat shafted through him when he remembered how those full lips had aroused him the previous night. He'd seen her outer beauty the first time he'd laid eyes on her. Smooth, flawless skin, small turned-up nose, big brown eyes—the combination was a package that could turn a man into a quivering mass of locked-and-loaded testosterone.

But he'd learned she was beautiful on the inside, too. She'd taken his daughter under her wing at a time when Kendra was insecure, confused, and scared about the future. How many women would do that?

As he studied her face, he noticed the shadows beneath her eyes, highlighted by her high, sculpted cheekbones. She'd told him several times that this was a very busy time for her. Was she working too hard?

A sensation of protectiveness expanded inside him. It wasn't unfamiliar; he felt it for his girls. But it was different. A man for his woman? Wow, that thought got his adrenaline pumping.

He pulled the covers more securely around her naked body and a wry thought occurred to him. At least he wasn't a do-as-I-say-not-as-I-do kind of father. He had feelings for the woman he'd slept with. He just wasn't sure what they were.

The insistent throbbing in his groin was proof that he wanted to make love to her again. But his gaze was drawn to the circles under her eyes and he didn't want to disturb her sleep.

Carefully, he slipped out of bed and slid into a pair of sweats and a T-shirt. He went downstairs and put on a pot of coffee. While he waited for it to be ready, he leaned his elbows on the island, stared into the family room and listened. There were no sounds. No thumping overhead to signal Kendra's footsteps. No galumphing down the stairs because she was late for school. No phone ringing off the hook. No loud music vibrating the second story of the house.

Nothing but damn peace and quiet.

And this is how it would be if she went away to college.

He remembered Thea teasing him about not being ready for his daughter to leave home and he'd assured her he could picture it clearly. There was a part of him looking forward to the break in 24/7 responsibility. But he had to admit he hadn't really known what an empty nest would feel like. He did now. And it felt weird.

"Good morning."

"Hey, sleepyhead." He smiled as Thea walked into the kitchen.

She'd put on his navy-colored terry-cloth robe and the abundance of thick material only made her look smaller and more fragile. His protective urge jabbed him again as surely as her elbow had just a little while ago.

He went to her and put his hands at her waist. Lowering his head, he kissed her and felt a sublime satisfaction when she shivered and sighed. "How did you sleep?"

"Good." She thought for a moment and added, "Better than I have in a long time."

"I'm glad." He traced the shadows beneath her left eye. "You need to work on getting rid of these."

"No. I just need to spread on the concealer with a palette knife."

"I think you look beautiful without makeup."

She grinned. "Silver-tongued devil."

"Busted."

He noticed the coffee had stopped dripping and went to get a mug. "Want some?"

She shook her head. "No caffeine. Remember?"

"Yeah. Right." He poured the strong, black brew into his mug and took a sip. "You don't know what you're missing. Guaranteed to put hair on your chest."

Her gaze dropped to his chest. "And a fine job it's done on you." Her grin faded and she said, "You were looking awfully pensive about something when I came in."

He set his coffee on the island and folded his arms over his chest as he leaned back against the cooktop. Thea stood with the island between them and he wondered if she was distancing herself on purpose. He knew last night's passion had caught her off guard. It had him too. He hadn't meant for things to get out of control like that. But he couldn't regret what happened and didn't want her to, either.

"Earth to Scott."

"Hmm?" He met her gaze. "Oh. Why was I looking thoughtful. I was thinking how quiet the house is with Kendra gone."

"Surely this isn't the first time. Hasn't she spent the night with friends?"

He nodded. "But this is different. Her going away to college is looming over me."

"Let me see if I've got this straight. She's facing the

leap from high school to college, but this is all about you?"

"Of course."

She leaned her elbows on the island and rested her chin in her hands. "Might I point out that you wanted her to go away to school? To have the total college experience by living on campus the way her older sister is?"

"If I'd known you were the kind of woman who actually listened to me and then throws my words back in my face—"

"Yes?"

"I'd have been more careful about what I said."

She laughed. "I'm just playing devil's advocate."

There was nothing devilish about her. She looked like an angel, even though her hair was sexily tousled and traces of a seriously satisfied woman lingered in her brown eyes.

"I guess I thought the feelings would be the same as when I sent Gail off to school. But they're not. Because I still had Ken. Now I'm actually looking at an empty nest."

"I thought you wanted to downsize."

"I think it's being forced on me because my rebellious children insist on growing up."

She moved around the island until she was no more than a foot away. There was a soft, tentative, tender sort of expression on her face that made her even more beautiful.

"Scott? You obviously care very much about your girls. And you're a terrific parent. You've done a wonderful job with them under circumstances that were less than ideal. Single parents everywhere could take lessons from you."

His eyebrows shot up at her praise. "Wow. I thought

you weren't going to feed my ego any more. You make me sound like a candidate for canonization."

She lifted one delicate shoulder swathed in the robe that was too big for her. "Can't help it. You're a good man doing a good job. And I have a feeling you don't get enough pats on the back."

"You can say that again."

She moved beside him and patted his back with her small hand. His skin burned even through the material of his shirt. "There."

"Thanks." He noticed when her expression turned thoughtful. "Speaking of pensive—"

"Hmm?"

"What's on your mind? I can see the wheels turning and if you don't spit it out, there's going to be a power drain in Santa Clarita."

She laughed. "I don't know. I just had a silly thought."

"Want to share?"

"I was just wondering. You're obviously going to miss Kendra when she leaves home. It occurred to me—have you ever thought about having more children?"

He shook his head. "To start again with two o'clock feedings, diapers. Teething. Nursing them through colds and the flu. Worrying about juggling child care and work. Worrying about everything…. I don't think so."

"You've had basic training. This time you'd bring seasoning and skill, knowledge and maturity to the experience."

"I've learned that life is always a trade-off. As much as I'd like to keep my girls small and run interference for them, protect them from all the bad stuff in life, they grew up and are eager to see what the world is all about. The trade-off is that now it's my turn to do what I missed out on when I took on responsibility too young."

"But you wouldn't have an empty nest," she said in a small voice. "Another child would—"

"No way."

His reaction was instinctive, straight from the gut. And the words must have come out sharper than he'd intended because Thea looked shocked and backed away. The startled expression on her face compelled him to explain.

"Sorry. Didn't mean to sound harsh. Apparently you struck a nerve. I just don't want more children, Thea. I'm very sure about that."

Thea's eyes grew wide and she looked shell-shocked. "I s-see."

Why did he feel as if he were the slimeball who just shot Bambi's mother? Irritation laced through him. He couldn't shake the sensation that he'd somehow let her down. That he'd disappointed her. Which meant she was judging him. And that wasn't fair. He'd gone through hell and tried to do the right thing. And she'd said herself that he'd done a good job. He'd had his two-point-whatever children and anyone who'd traveled the same path he had would probably feel the same way.

The truth hit him between the eyes. She hadn't traveled the same path. Her husband had died and she had no children. Did she want them? She was still a very young woman. How did she feel about kids? His gut clenched.

"Look, Thea, I—"

"Wow, it's getting late," she said, glancing at the clock on the microwave. "I have a bridal shower to get ready for. I better get dressed. Excuse me."

Scott ran his fingers through his hair as he watched

her hurry from the room. So much for the postcoital glow. It was nice while it lasted. He was so out of the loop on this man/woman thing. Maybe it would have been better if he'd lied to her.

He shook his head. If telling lies was a prerequisite for a relationship, then he was destined to be alone. That just wasn't his style.

Thea was back a few minutes later dressed in the clothes she'd worn yesterday. She briefly met his gaze before hers skittered away. "I'll work up those figures for you on the party."

"Okay." He moved toward her. "I'll call you—"

"I'm going to be out all day."

He followed her to the front door. When she opened it and started to leave, he curved his fingers around her upper arm to stop her. She glanced up, her eyes shadowed and questioning.

He leaned down and brushed his lips over hers. "Have a good day. Drive careful. You look tired. Don't work too hard."

"You don't have to worry about me."

"I know," he said.

As he watched her get in her car and drive away, it struck him that not worrying about her was easier said than done.

Chapter Ten

After the bridal shower, Thea ladled the remaining iced tea—passion fruit flavor—into a container. As if she needed a reminder that she'd engaged in the fruits of passion. That she'd spent the night with Scott, tangled in his sheets and in his arms. It was so nice while it lasted. As she continued to empty the contents of the decorative jar, she remembered in painful detail Scott's adamant declaration about children.

Connie appeared beside her with the leftover shrimp dish and fruit salad. "Are you okay?"

"Yeah. Just moving slow. Sorry."

"No problem. Everyone is gone, including the party hostess. I told her we'd lock up when we were finished putting the house back together."

"Good." Thea was glad it was just the two of them, although she'd have preferred to be alone.

"I'm going to strip the linens off the dining room table and put the chairs back."

"Okay. I'll take care of these leftovers and leave them in the fridge."

Thea took some of the disposable containers she always brought with her and scooped the shrimp into one, then labeled it. She did the same with the fruit and put the bowls away. It was part of the service she offered. Thea Bell toils for you and makes your life a little easier.

If only someone would do that for her. She'd felt as if life was finally starting to go her way when the IVF was successful. Then she met Scott. It had been downhill ever since, capped by sex with him. No, that was the high point. Even though all the signs had been apparent, she'd harbored some misguided notion that he might be open to the possibility of another child—her child. Until he'd told her in no uncertain terms how he felt, she hadn't even realized the hope was there. Because she didn't dare to hope any more.

"Thea, are you all right?" There was sincere concern in her friend's voice.

She turned away from the open refrigerator. "Yes. Why?"

"Because you've been standing there with the fridge door open staring off into space. That's not like you. In fact, you haven't been yourself all day. So talk to me. You know I won't let up until you do."

Thea shut the door and released a long breath. "Okay. I'm not okay."

Connie was beside her in a flash. "What's wrong? Is it the baby?"

"The baby's fine. I slept with Scott Matthews last night," she said in a rush. Then she looked at her friend whose expression went from worried to shocked to smug in three seconds flat.

She held up her hand. "High-five, girlfriend."

"No. I should bend over and let you kick me in the fanny. It was probably the dumbest thing I've ever done. It was a mistake."

"Why? Was he bad in bed? Did he not know what he was doing?"

Thea shivered at the memory of what Scott had done to her, how he'd made her come alive with his hands, his mouth, his body. "No. He knew what he was doing, all right."

"Then I don't get it. What part of it was a mistake?"

"The whole thing. It never should have happened. We were friends. And now…"

"You're friends who had sex."

"It's not that simple. Don't you see?" Thea held out her hand in a frustrated, helpless gesture. "We were intimate."

"Yeah. That's kind of the point of sex. A man and a woman getting intimate."

"You are the most exasperating woman. If I didn't like you so much—" She shook her head, but couldn't suppress a small smile.

"I'm not exasperating. I'm clueless. The man is a hunk and a half. He's gainfully employed."

"And then some," Thea agreed.

"He's interested in you. You're obviously attracted to him. More important, you like him. What is the problem?"

"He doesn't want any more children," Thea said miserably. "That's a deal breaker."

"It would be if he really meant it."

"Oh, he did."

"Lots of people say it. Including me. But if the situation arises, you roll with it," Connie said.

"Not him."

"How can you be so sure?"

"He told me so." Shaking her head, she blew out a long breath. "He took on heavy responsibilities at a very young age. Now it's his turn to do his own thing. And that doesn't include another baby."

"But, T—"

Thea held up her hand. "You should have seen his face when he talked about all the negatives—two o'clock feedings, flu and fevers, teething. He loves his children but he doesn't want the responsibility that comes with a baby."

"Did you tell him you're pregnant?"

Thea shook her head. "I got out of there as fast as I could."

"You should tell him."

"There's no need to. Now that I know how he feels, there's no chance of taking anything between us to the next level."

"I think you're wrong, Thea. There's always a chance."

"Speaking of fevers," she said, reaching over to touch the back of her hand to her friend's forehead.

Connie ducked away. "I'm serious. And completely in my right mind. He obviously likes you a lot. Maybe more than like. If I'm right, and he finds out you and a baby are a package deal, he might accept it."

"I don't want 'acceptance' for this baby," Thea said sharply. She meant that with all her heart. "David would have loved being a father, but that wasn't meant to be. Now it's my responsibility to raise our child the way he would have wanted. That doesn't include letting a man into my life who would simply tolerate the child I'm carrying."

"But if you tell him—"

"No. It's my personal business," Thea said. "And there's no reason now to share it with Scott."

"Even though you're friends?"

"We're not that close."

"I don't know," Connie said, tucking a strand of copper-colored hair behind her ear. "Sex, by definition, means you get pretty close."

"You know what I mean," Thea said, just this side of exasperated. "Besides, we won't be having sex again. I intend to let him know it was a mistake. Hopefully that won't impact his feelings when I make an offer on his house. And he indicated he's interested in my place. He's condo and I'm single-family home. We're wrong for each other and at completely different places in our lives. It was a terrible mistake to let things get out of hand like they did."

"Maybe. But once you've crossed over, it's hard to go back," her friend pointed out.

Especially when one didn't want to, Thea thought. But the bigger mistake would be in letting things go on knowing how he felt.

"I'll just have to find a way to make sure he gets the message. After our real estate deals are finished, any association with Scott Matthews will be finished, too."

"Don't be too sure," Connie warned.

Thea ignored her. There couldn't be a game if only one person participated. Scott was a bright guy. Smart, handsome, tender, loving, strong, reliable—

She put the brakes on that train of thought before she derailed her own best intentions. He was a really terrific guy who deserved to find an equally terrific woman to care about. Someone who met his criteria. And she wasn't the one.

It didn't matter that the thought of him with anyone else made her heart hurt.

Scott dialed Thea's number without looking it up. How quickly he'd memorized it, he thought. That happened when you phoned a woman over and over because she hadn't returned your calls even after you'd left numerous messages.

"Hello?"

Finally, he thought, muting the TV as he sat up straighter on the sofa. "Hi. Thea? It's Scott."

"Oh. Hello," she said, breathlessly. It sounded as if she'd just come in and raced to the phone.

Or just finished making love.

That thought generated a shaft of heat that shot straight to his groin. At the same time, just hearing her voice produced a yearning so deep inside him it was almost painful. That had happened almost as fast as memorizing her phone number. And wasn't that the pits. The last time he'd needed a woman, his whole life had turned upside down when she'd walked out. He'd promised himself never to need anyone again.

"I guess you've been busy," he said casually.

"Yes." The sound of crackling came over the phone, as if she were setting bags down. "Why?"

"Because you didn't return any of my messages."

"Oh. Yeah."

"Or have you been avoiding me?"

He winced when the words came out. He'd just finished warning himself not to get sucked in. Now he was quizzing her about why she hadn't called him back. Stupid move, Matthews, he thought.

"Why would I do that?"

Classic avoidance technique. Answer a question

with another question. "I'm not sure. Maybe because things are moving kind of fast between us."

"You mean because we—you know."

He heard the embarrassment in her voice and could almost see the blush he knew would be coloring the flawless skin of her cheeks.

"Yeah. That."

"No—I mean, yes, things did move fast."

"I refuse to say I'm sorry it happened, Thea. And I hope you're not sorry, either."

"You have nothing to be sorry for. It takes two to tango, as they say. No one forced me."

He noticed she hadn't said she wasn't sorry. "So that's not why you haven't returned my calls?"

There was a telling silence before she said, "Of course not."

"Good, then—"

"Did you get the estimated cost of food per person for Kendra's party that I faxed to your office?"

"Yes. Why?"

"I thought maybe you had a question about it," she said.

"No. It's fine."

"Good. All right, then, if there's nothing else—"

"Whoa. Wait a minute."

"Yes?"

"What's with you?"

"I don't know what you mean," she hedged.

"The heck you don't. First you don't return my calls. Then you change the subject to business. Now you're trying to get me off the phone. You are avoiding me."

"Why would I do that?"

For the same reason he'd been avoiding emotional entanglements since his wife had left him and their two little girls. "Because you're afraid of being hurt again after losing your husband," he said.

There was a loud sigh on the other end of the line. "There could be some truth to that," she admitted.

"You can't run forever, Thea."

"Wanna bet?"

"Seriously, sooner or later you have to take a chance and get back on that horse."

"And you know this because you've had so much experience taking chances?" she asked sarcastically. "Do I file that advice under, 'Takes one to know one'?"

"Touché. I've been reluctant to dip my toe in the cold water of relationships," he said. "But after meeting you I find that I'm inclined to want to dive in."

"It's all about sex, isn't it?"

"No." And he truly meant that. Mostly. "Although I can't tell a lie. I'm all in favor of sex. With you."

She sighed again. "Look, Scott—"

"I'm not going to like this, am I?"

"I couldn't say. But I can't tell a lie, either."

"Sure you can."

"No," she said with a small laugh. "Since we met—"

"And made love," he interjected.

"That, too, I've realized I'm not ready to take a chance and get back on the horse. Or dive into the waters of a relationship. Or whatever else you want to call it. And to be honest, I'm not sure I ever will be."

"There's that honesty thing again," he grumbled.

He didn't especially like the way this was going and wished he'd let her continue avoiding him.

"I don't know any other way to be."

That was refreshing anyway. He'd lived with a woman who told him what he wanted to hear until the day she said she couldn't stand her life and was leaving him. But Thea's truth was only marginally better.

"Look, Scott, I just want to be fair to you," she said, filling the silence.

"I don't know what's fair. All I know is that there's something going on between us. Or am I the only one who feels it?"

"I feel strongly that the wisest course of action is to nip this thing in the bud. Before either of us realizes we want more than the other can give."

Scott wasn't sure what he wanted except he knew he didn't want to simply end it. Thea Bell was a pretty amazing woman and it didn't feel right to walk away from her just like that. Wasn't it just his luck that the first woman he'd met who made him want to take the risk was afraid to go there with him.

"Look, Thea, let me take you out to dinner and we can talk about this."

"I don't think so, Scott."

He would bet if he brought up Kendra's party she'd change her tune. Since the day he'd caught her cooking in his kitchen, she'd backed away from the personal and taken cover behind the professional.

"What about my house? Didn't you want to make an offer?"

"Yes, but I still have to sell my condo."

"What if I want to buy it?"

The silence on the other end of the line told him her eyes widened and she was blinking in surprise.

"Do you?" she asked.

"It's exactly what I pictured myself in after the girls were gone."

"Then we should get Joyce to write up offers on each other's property."

But that would mean I can't see you, he thought. He also suspected if he pushed any harder, he'd push her away. That was the last thing he wanted. "Okay," he agreed.

He didn't think he could persuade her to go out with him just yet, but he didn't want to hang up without knowing when he would see her again. "What's the next step for the party?"

"When you know the number of guests who will be attending, I'll reserve tables and chairs. Then I'll need to take a look at the backyard and figure out where to set everything up."

"Okay. I'll sit down with Ken when she comes home from UCLA and we'll finalize the guest list."

"Good. If that's all, Scott, I have to run. I'll talk to you when you've got all that information."

"Okay, good—"

He heard the click and stared at the receiver. When it sank in that she'd hung up on him, anger churned in his gut. He should be relieved that she didn't seem to want anything serious between them. But he wasn't. She'd basically told him that if not for Kendra's party, she would have nothing to do with him.

And he didn't like it one little bit.

Chapter Eleven

Scott slammed the phone down and ran his fingers through his hair. "Son of a—"

"Dad?"

He looked up. Kendra and Gail were standing in the family room staring at him. He hadn't even heard them come in. Thea was some distraction. No wonder they named every other hurricane after a woman.

"Hi," he said, then released a long breath.

"Something wrong?" Kendra asked.

He glanced at the phone. "It's no big deal."

So much for not being able to tell a lie. He didn't need a shrink to tell him his over-the-top reaction meant it was a very big deal.

"So," he said, looking from one daughter to the other, "how was your weekend?"

"Awesome," Kendra said. She was beaming.

He hadn't seen her this happy since she'd scored the

winning goal for her soccer team and sent them to the playoffs.

But he had to be cool and let her open up on her own. "Oh?" he asked, looking at Gail.

"It was great, Dad. I showed her the campus and where my classes are. Then there was a—"

"Whoa. Time out." Kendra dropped her backpack in the family room and walked into the kitchen, straight to the refrigerator. "It's my orientation," she said sliding a good-natured glare in her sister's direction. "I'll tell him."

"I'm listening," he said.

"Dad, it was so cool. There was a meeting of all incoming freshmen. I thought it would be lame, but Gail made me go. She said she did it and met some cool people. There was an exhibition basketball game at Pauley Pavilion."

"And?" he prompted.

Kendra popped the top on her soda can and took a sip. "I had the best time. I met a ton of kids who are starting classes in the fall."

"Are any of these people guys?"

"Da-ad." She rolled her eyes.

"It's my job to ask," he explained.

"Okay. Yes, some of them were guys. And they seemed really nice."

"Don't worry, Dad." Gail sat down beside him. "I already gave her the 4-1-1 on not trusting every college guy she meets. It's cool."

"Okay." He met Kendra's gaze and she nodded slightly, letting him know she'd explained her unfortunate experience to her sister. Her eyes narrowed slightly and he figured she was warning him to let it drop. He got the message.

"So where did you stay?" he asked.

"In Gail's dorm. It's pretty small," Kendra explained.

"Like living in a cardboard box," Gail grumbled.

His youngest nodded eagerly. "But if you're organized, there's lots of storage in the closet. And space under the bed."

"When's the last time you saw any space under your bed? Or anywhere else in your room for that matter?" Scott teased her.

"Don't start, Dad. Let the euphoria wear off naturally," Kendra advised.

"Okay." He looked at the glow on her face. "I guess this means you're going away to college?"

"Yeah."

"I'm not sure I want you to," he admitted.

He'd realized how much he would miss Kendra the morning after making love to Thea. Just thinking Thea's name tied his gut in knots. He didn't get her at all. But while she was there, he'd gotten how much he was going to miss the energy his youngest daughter brought into this house. Then he remembered— this was the house that Thea was going to buy. Somehow, the woman had woven herself into the fabric of his life.

"Now you *don't* want me to go?"

He shrugged. "I missed the heck out of you."

Kendra looked surprised. "You missed me?"

He nodded. "Like crazy."

Gail took a sip of her water. "See, I told you, sis."

"Told her what?" Scott asked.

"That you loved her and she was nuts."

"That, I get. But why do you think so?" he asked, grinning when Ken huffed loudly.

"She thinks you didn't want her. That you wished she'd never been born," Gail explained.

He stared at his youngest daughter. "Why would you think such a thing, Kendra?"

She looked down at her sneakers and rubbed the top of one against the calf of her leg. "I heard you tell Uncle Mike. You said you wished I'd never been born. That it would be easier. It was right after Mom left."

Scott couldn't have been more shocked if she'd slugged him in the stomach. He couldn't have said that. She must have misunderstood. "I don't know what you overheard, but the truth is that after you were born, I couldn't imagine my life without you in it. I fell in love with you the moment I laid eyes on you."

She nodded. "Thea told me the same thing."

Thea. She'd somehow become important in their lives. But he tucked thoughts of her away for later, when he could sort them out. "Ken, your mom and I had a complicated relationship. After you were born I thought things were fine, then found out I was wrong. It was a rough time. But whatever you heard me say to Uncle Mike, I'm sure it wasn't that I never wanted you."

Kendra nodded. "It's okay, Dad. I understand better now."

"So we're clear. You don't think I wish you'd never been born?"

"Nope." She reached over and gave him a hug, then pulled back.

"Good."

It was possible that with her own pregnancy scare, she had put herself in his shoes as much as she could and was able to imagine a little of what he'd gone through. When Scott met her gaze, there was no hostility in it, thank goodness. Maybe this was the silver lining of that whole fiasco with the weasel who'd used her. Although he'd still like to rip the jerk's head off for hurting his little girl.

"I love you guys," he said. He hated the fact that life was changing and the three of them weren't together all the time. These two were his family and he loved them with everything he had. He'd die for them.

"I love you, too, Dad," the girls said together.

Smiling, he glanced from one daughter to the other. Kendra was dark-haired; Gail's hair was streaked with blond. One was blue-eyed; the other's eyes were green like her mother's. His gut clenched at the thought. He'd tried to give his girls a solid foundation and understanding of right and wrong so they'd never turn out like their mother. That time had nearly brought him to his knees and he'd sworn never to trust a woman again. Somehow Thea had sneaked past that promise. So maybe she'd done him a favor by shutting down things between them.

"Earth to Dad." Gail was moving her hand in front of his face to get his attention.

"Hmm?" he said blinking.

"You look like you did when you wanted to beat up Doug Satterfield." Kendra looked horrified and instantly clamped her hand over her mouth.

"Is that the toad's name?" he asked.

"Dad, if you really love me, you'll forget I said that."

"I can't promise to forget. But I won't do anything about it unless you give me the green light."

"Not in this lifetime," she said, looking relieved. "But what's wrong? You look like someone dumped you."

"Dating happens before dumping," Gail pointed out. "And you don't date. Do you?"

If you didn't count the deposit he'd given Thea for

the graduation party, he hadn't spent money on her. He wasn't sure if making love to a woman could be classified as dating and tried to decide how to answer the question.

"It's Thea," Kendra guessed. "Are you dating her?"

"No," he said. Technically that was the truth. She'd essentially told him to take a flying leap.

"But you want to?" Kendra guessed again.

Did he? He'd gotten a glimpse of life post-child-rearing and it loomed lonely. On the other hand, his spectator seat had included a view with and without Thea. The outlook with her had been far more pleasant and exciting.

But he didn't want to open that door and have it slammed in his face again. So the answer to his youngest daughter's question was, "I don't know."

"If you like Thea, don't give up," Gail advised. "Remember, it's better to have loved and lost than never to have loved at all."

Kendra snorted in disgust. "Spoken by someone who's never been through a major heartbreak."

"Yes, I have," her sister shot back. "Remember Greg Smith?"

"No."

"Well, it's not important that you do. *I* remember the pain of rejection." She glanced at the clock on the microwave. "More important, I have to get back to school. I have an early class in the morning." She smiled at her sister. "In a few short months, we'll be there together."

"I can't wait," Kendra agreed.

Scott watched the girls hug, grateful their relationship was so close. Gail would watch out for her little sister. She gave him a hug and whispered in his ear, "Perseverance. Wear her down."

She left and Kendra went upstairs to her room. And he was alone.

"Better get used to it," he said to himself.

He thought about what Gail had said—better to have loved and lost. That was the biggest load of crap he'd ever heard. He and Kendra—and Thea—were all casualties of love. Pain was not better.

He'd give anything for his daughter to have never been hurt and disillusioned the way she'd been. The experience had almost impacted her college plans.

And Thea. The man she'd loved had died and she was still dealing with it. He'd bet she didn't buy into the saying any more than he did. He'd wager she wished she hadn't lost the man she'd loved.

And Scott figured it was a no-brainer that he'd rather not have his relationship scars. If he'd never cared about his ex-wife, there wouldn't *be* any scars. He and Thea were damaged goods.

Tonight she'd told him she didn't want to pursue anything of a personal nature.

He didn't, either. He didn't want to take another chance.

There was only one problem with that.

All he could think about was Thea Bell. What was he going to do if he couldn't get her out of his mind?

Thea filed the folder with her accepted offer on Scott's house. Then she started another one for the deal on her condo with his offer inside. They were in escrow—actually switching spaces. There would be no living with Connie's ego when she found out. To put her ego and meddling tendencies in line, Thea would have to share that she'd put the lid on anything personal between herself and Scott.

Even though it had been a week since they'd last spoken on the phone, thoughts of him made her sad. Shouldn't she be over that by now? Shouldn't she be over missing him? The fact that she wasn't and she did, miss him that is, proved she'd been right to end it. Things between them had escalated at the speed of light. If she hadn't put a stop to it, they'd have gone beyond the point of no return. That would have been a disaster.

Her focus now had to be the baby growing inside her. She put her palms over her still flat belly. "You're not growing fast enough, little one."

She went into her living room and took a throw pillow from the couch. Stuffing it beneath her T-shirt, she tried to imagine how it would be when the baby was that big and she could feel movement. She stood in front of the entry mirror to see herself.

Grinning at her image, she said, "I never thought I'd say this, but I can't wait to be as big as a house."

Suddenly her doorbell rang, making her jump. "I'm not expecting anyone," she said to herself. "Maybe it's Connie."

She looked through the peephole and was startled again. Scott Matthews stood there. Instantly her pulse cranked up in direct proportion to the joy she experienced at the sight of him. How pathetic was she? The bell rang again, more insistently this time. If she knew what was good for her, she would ignore it. But the fact was she couldn't resist the temptation to see him up close. When her awkward belly brushed the door, she removed the pillow from beneath her shirt and set it on the table in the entryway. Then she slid the dead bolt off.

After opening the door, she said, "Hi, Scott."

"Thea." He met her gaze and his own was sizzling with emotion. "I need to talk to you."

"If it's about our real estate deal, I'd prefer you direct any problems to Joyce." It was so hard to turn the conversation to business when her nerve endings were snapping with excitement and energy was humming through her.

"It's not about that."

"Then what?"

She thought she'd successfully sidestepped an emotional confrontation, but the expression on his face told her differently. It was common knowledge that the average single man looked for an excuse to avoid entanglements. It was completely unfair that she'd met one who wouldn't take the out she'd given him.

"It's about needing to see you," he said.

Her insides melted like sugar glaze over warm cake. All of a sudden, she couldn't be sorry he hadn't listened to her.

He moved in closer and stopped so that their bodies were an inch apart, but not touching. She loved the way he smelled. When she breathed in the wonderful masculine scent of him, it burrowed inside her and set off a chain reaction, a heat-activated response.

"It's about not being able to stop thinking about you," he said, his voice hoarse and rough with feeling.

"Oh?"

"And I tried," he said, anger lacing the words. "I tried my damnedest to put you out of my mind." His voice was low and rough and exciting.

"I see."

"The hell you do. Do you think I'd be here if I had a choice? Do you think I like running into a brick wall?" He shook his head and a muscle jumped in his cheek.

"I can't think about anything but you. You're in my thoughts when I'm dreaming and when I'm wide awake."

The anger and frustration in his gaze startled her with their intensity. His words were like salve to her shattered soul. She caught her breath at the power of the passion emanating from him. Was she really and truly responsible for his profound feelings? It had been so long since she'd felt wanted and, most especially, *needed*.

"Scott, I don't know what to say—"

He cupped her left cheek in his palm. "Me, either."

She looked into his eyes, saw the tension in the line of his mouth and felt the weight of everything separating them. She'd been such a fool to think this moment would never come. This was the point of no return. He had to know about the baby.

"Scott, there's something I have to tell you—"

He touched a finger to her lips to silence her. "Didn't you just say you don't know *what* to say? In my opinion, talking is highly overrated."

He removed his finger, then lowered his head and with exquisite tenderness, touched his lips to hers. Thea couldn't agree with him more about talking. Her heart stopped momentarily, then thumped painfully against the wall of her chest. His lips were soft and warm, and he nibbled hers for several seconds before nipping a spot just beside the corner of her mouth. Her fully charged nerve endings combusted on contact, sending all coherent thought down the tubes.

All she could think about was the way her skin was sensitized to his touch. Shivers and tingles danced over her body. It felt as if a boulder were sitting squarely on her chest, as if she couldn't draw enough air into her lungs.

And she didn't want to. She wanted only to concentrate on the feelings he generated inside her. She needed to touch and be touched. Like the last time she'd been with Scott, everything spiraled out of control as soon as he brushed his lips over hers.

He pulled her into his strong arms and trailed nibbling kisses over her cheek and jaw to that place he'd discovered just beneath her ear. When he touched the tip of his tongue there, it was like a lovely electric shock. Sensation arced through her and all she could think was that she wanted more. His tender touch filled the emptiness inside her and torched the banked fire of her need. Woulds, shoulds and coulds were burned away by the heat his mouth generated and the pleasure evoked by his warm hands as they moved tenderly up and down her spine.

He pulled back, his breathing ragged. "I didn't mean for that to happen. But I saw you and—" He shrugged as his mouth curved up on one side. "I just couldn't help myself. I'm sorry."

"I'm not."

And she meant that with every fiber of her being. Even if it damned her to hell for eternity, she could no more deny herself the sweetness of being with this man than she could refuse air to breathe.

"No?"

Instead of wasting her breath with words, she smiled and took his hand, leading him upstairs to her bedroom. The walls were pale pink, the bed skirt and quilt were covered with roses in variegated shades of crimson. An arch of dried flowers was the focal point of a grouping of needlepoint blossoms on the wall above the bed. Everything about the room spoke of femininity, yet she'd never felt like a complete woman in it.

Until now. With this man.

Scott took the hem of her T-shirt and she raised her arms, encouraging him to lift it over her head. Then he undid the button at the waist of her jeans and slid down the zipper. She pushed the material over her legs and stepped out of them. Too late she realized her bra and panties were plain white cotton, not the stuff of seduction. What she wouldn't give for a matched set of red satin. Then it ceased to matter as he looked at her and his gaze grew hot.

"You're so beautiful," he said, the words hardly more than a breath of air.

"You don't have to tell me that."

"Would you rather I lie and say you're so homely you'd have to sneak up on a glass of water?"

She laughed. For some reason that reassured her more completely than flowery words and practiced phrases. He was telling her the simple truth the way he saw it. Which meant when he looked at her, he saw beauty.

Her heart filled to overflowing with emotions she couldn't name. Then he reached behind her, unhooked her bra, and she didn't want to think at all. As the material slid away and the cool air touched her breasts, so did his gaze.

"Beautiful," he said again.

He reached around her to the bed and yanked down the quilt, blanket and sheet. When he pulled his shirt over his head without bothering to unbutton it, her heart beat so furiously she thought it would fly from her chest. He slid his feet from his shoes and then went to work on his pants. Fascinated, she watched the ripple of muscles across his chest and arms as he unbuckled his belt, then pushed his jeans and briefs down over muscular thighs and calves. His erection sprang free and her breath caught in her throat. Fearing her trembling legs wouldn't hold her, she sat on the bed and then moved to the center, making room for him.

The mattress dipped from his weight as he put one knee on it then slid closer and settled beside her—the first man ever in this bed. In this room. It felt so right that Scott was the one.

When she shivered, he pulled her close and brought the sheet up over them. "Better?"

"Yes," she whispered. "But only because you're here."

He grinned as he pressed her even closer, nestling her naked breasts to the wall of his chest. "Shared body heat is an amazing thing."

"I couldn't agree more." She liked the rough texture of his chest hair on the tender skin of her breasts. Was there anything that could make a woman feel more feminine than that?

He reached down and slid her panties off. Then he rubbed his large palm over the dip of her waist and down the length of her thigh. In the wake of his touch, heat exploded. Liquid warmth spread through her, settling in her center, readying her body to accept him. And that answered her question. A man's possession could definitely bring out the woman in her.

He took her lips with his own and kissed her thoroughly, with exquisite tenderness. She opened, admitting him inside, savoring the invasion of his tongue that imitated the motion of lovemaking. She traced the roof of his mouth, taking profound female satisfaction when he groaned deep in his throat. His chest rose and fell rapidly.

"Wow," he said, struggling to catch his breath. "Lady, you pack a wallop."

"You're no slouch yourself," she breathed. Then she touched the tip of her tongue to his earlobe.

"Oh, God—" he said.

She felt his erection pressing into her belly and again felt the power of her femininity. It seemed the most important thing in the world to touch him, to know the texture of him, to feel the essence of his maleness in the palm of her hand.

"Thea—" His voice was raspy and strained.

For so long she'd existed in a haze, but Scott had brought her out of the clouds and into the light. She'd felt the weight of too many things out of her control. Now, with him, she felt as if she could take command. When he rolled to his back, it was as if he could read her mind. She knelt beside him, then settled herself over him.

Groaning with satisfaction, he put his big hands on her hips and guided her, showing her the rhythm, urging her faster. Her breathing kept pace and her heart hammered as if she were running the hundred-yard dash. Pressure built inside her until she felt like a volcano about to erupt.

He reached out a hand searching for and finding the nub of her femininity pressed to the shaft of his masculinity. Her engorged bundle of nerve endings was exquisitely sensitive to his touch. He stroked her gently until the pressure released into a thousand points of light and she collapsed against his chest.

When she recovered enough, he urged her hips into motion again and seconds later, he stilled her as he groaned his own release.

It seemed an eternity until she could move, but when she stirred, he nestled her against his side with her cheek on his chest. The musky, life-affirming scent of sex drifted in the air. They were skin to skin and the warmth of him wrapped around her. With the taste of him still on her lips, she savored the rise and fall of his chest, the sound of his breathing. The power of the moment hit her. All her senses told her she wasn't alone. The thought brought tears to her eyes.

Because it felt so good.

And because it was way past time for her to tell him about her baby.

He kissed her forehead. "Thea, I hope you know I didn't come here just for…you know."

"I know," she said, her stomach knotting. "You came here to talk. And I agree we need to. Can you stay?"

"The girls are due home soon. I wish I could. But I need to be there when they get back."

"I understand."

"I don't want to be a do-as-I-say-not-as-I-do kind of dad."

"I know. But you've got a few minutes?"

It was time to tell him everything and see where they were going with this crazy whatever-it-was between them. She knew now he had feelings for her. Maybe, just maybe, they were strong enough to bear what she had to say.

He glanced at the clock on the nightstand. "Not really. I have to go." He threw back the sheet and sat up. "I'm taking the girls to brunch tomorrow morning before Gail goes back to school. Would you like to join us?"

What she wanted was to run her hands over his back and memorize every hard angle and muscular contour. But she didn't. "I think it would be best if I didn't go along," she said.

"The girls wouldn't mind. They like you."

"I'm glad."

"In fact they're the reason I came over tonight. Last weekend they encouraged me not to give up on you."

"And it took you all week to decide they were right?" she teased.

"I may be slow," he admitted. "But once I make up my mind, look out." His expression turned sheepish. "That didn't sound right. I really did come here just to talk."

"I believe you." If she hadn't needed him so badly, that's probably all they would have done. "But you won't have many opportunities from now on to have them all to yourself. I'd love a rain check, though."

"You got it."

He slipped out of bed and dressed quickly as she lay on the bed watching him and loving every minute. When he was finished, he leaned over and ran his hand over her breast and to her abdomen, over the life growing there. She sucked in a breath as her chest tightened.

"I'll call you," he said.

"Okay."

Then he was gone. She wasn't a coward. Not completely. She should have told him. But he was looking forward to tomorrow with his girls. She wasn't certain if her news would cast a cloud over his day, but why take a chance.

A chance. She clung to the word with all her might. God wouldn't be so cruel. There was always a chance Scott cared enough that he wouldn't give up on her when she told him about her baby.

Chapter Twelve

Thea set a plate with soda crackers on the coffee table, then put her feet up on her couch and rested against the throw pillows. Morning sickness strikes again, she thought. Except it wasn't morning and it was after the first trimester, so shouldn't it be over? Her stomach rolled right over on that damn pregnancy glow.

She sighed as she patted her belly. "From everything I've read, little one, the hallmark of being a mother is to expect the unexpected. Thanks for the reminder." She closed her eyes against the nausea and said, "I think."

Connie had sent her home with specific orders to put her feet up. In fact, they were finished for the day, so Junior's timing was actually pretty good.

When her doorbell rang, she decided someone else's timing wasn't so good. Unless it was Scott. The last time she'd had an unexpected visitor, it was him. And he'd made such tender love to her, the memory of it made her heart ache to think about it.

With very little effort, she could fall for that man.

When the doorbell rang again, she sat up and swung her legs to the side. The thought of seeing him was about the only thing that could get her off this couch.

She peeked through the peephole and recognized Kendra. The last time the teen had dropped in, there was a crisis in the Matthews household. This was becoming a habit, a thought that pleased her very much. Not the crisis part, but the fact that the girl felt she could come to her.

She threw the dead bolt and opened the door. "Hi, there. Is everything all right?"

"Yeah. The best." Kendra smiled. "Didn't my dad tell you when he was here the other night?"

The other night when her father had been here, they hadn't talked about much. Their mouths had been otherwise occupied. Thea felt the heat rushing to her face and hoped the teen didn't notice.

"He said he was taking you and Gail to brunch. But that was about it. How was orientation?"

"Awesome," the teen said, grinning from ear to ear. "I met some cool kids. The campus is the best. I can't wait to go."

"So you're not afraid anymore?"

She shook her head. "And I have you to thank for talking me into giving it a try."

"No. You're the one who took the steps." She held out her arm. "Come in."

"I can't stay long." Kendra slung her backpack over one shoulder. "I stopped by your office, but Connie said you'd already left for the day. Are you okay?" she asked, looking closer.

"Fine. A little tired. I've been busy the last few weeks."

The girl looked uneasy. "Then I don't want to bother you."

Thea sat on the couch and patted the space beside her. "Sit. Tell me what's up. It's no bother."

"You might change your mind about that when I tell you."

"Let me be the judge. What can I do for you?"

Kendra took a big breath. "Mother's Day is coming up in a couple weeks."

"Yeah."

Thea was well aware. It would be her very first. But given Kendra's history with her mother, she couldn't imagine where she was going with this. Was she going to reach out to the woman who'd abandoned her?

"I want to surprise my dad with a party and I was hoping you'd help me pull it off."

"On Mother's Day?" she asked, surprised.

The teen twisted her fingers in her lap as an earnest expression crept into the blue eyes so like her father's. "The fact is, he's been both mother and father to me for as long as I can remember. I-I've been a pain in the neck to him lately and it's a way to say I'm sorry."

Thea reached over and squeezed her hand. "He loves you. No matter what."

"I know. In spite of everything. And he's always been there for me." She shrugged. "I guess there's something about going away to college. It feels final even though I know I'll see him a lot."

"It's a change," Thea agreed. "Everything will be different."

"That's for sure. But it feels like the right time to try and thank him for everything. I've been a big job and I want to do this in a big way."

"On Mother's Day."

"Yeah," she agreed. "Because he won't be expecting it. And I really, really need you to help me."

Thea smiled. Something about this girl always tugged at her heart. Was it because she was so much like her dad? Or that she'd seemed to be reaching out for something missing from her life? Either way, she was a sweetie. And the bottom line was Thea couldn't say no.

"Count me in," she said.

Kendra leaned over and hugged her. "Thank you."

"What can I do?"

"Help me plan the food. And we need a theme. I was hoping to have it at my grandparents' house so Dad won't know. And combine it with a Mother's Day celebration for my grandmother."

"So you're going to let her in on the surprise?"

"No, I want her to be surprised, too. I have a key to the house so you can set up. And I'll figure out a way to get everyone out of there."

"What about a movie?" Thea suggested. If the teenager couldn't pull that off, it would be déjà vu all over again when they walked in and found her cooking.

"Good idea," Kendra agreed.

"That would make it an evening event," she said, tapping her lip. Thea usually spent the morning with her own mother on that day, so there wasn't a conflict. "What kind of food do you want?"

"I'm not sure."

"Your dad likes Italian—"

"Yeah. Good idea."

"We could do stuffed shells or manicotti. Antipasto salad, garlic bread. And dessert. For how many people?"

"Just the family. Gail, me, Dad of course. My grandparents and Uncle Mike."

"A small celebration," Thea said.

"I can't afford more than that."

Thea hadn't even thought about charging her. When something didn't feel like business, it made her nervous. But that wasn't Kendra's problem. "Don't worry about the money."

"But I can't ask you to do this for free."

"We can work something out." Thea shrugged. "Actually, you can help me with everything. As I explained to your father, labor is the major expense."

Kendra raised one hand and put the other over her heart. "I swear I'll be your willing slave and promise to do whatever you tell me without complaint, whining, or eye-rolling."

Thea laughed as she pointed at her. "I'll hold you to that."

They talked for several more minutes, exchanging pertinent information. As they did, Thea noticed the sparkle in Kendra's eyes. She was different from the girl Thea had met a few months ago. She seemed happier and more confident. The result of a young girl whose father had given her space here and advice there. It was all about balance and Scott had pulled it off. Twice, when you counted Kendra's older sister. Thea put the date in her book and Kendra wrote down her grandparents' address.

The teen nodded eagerly. "You'll love Grammy and Poppy."

"I have no doubt." Children were a reflection of their parents, Thea realized. And Scott's mom and dad had raised a fine man.

After seeing Kendra out, she leaned against her door and sighed. He was a fine father, too. The kind any kid would be lucky to have.

She looked down and wondered about her own baby. He'd never know his father. Before undertaking the IVF, she'd rationalized that you couldn't miss what you'd never had. After meeting Scott and his girls, she wasn't so sure the rationale held up. Kendra missed her mother. Would her child miss his father? Would he turn out all right without one?

Scott had so much to offer—in every way. And he seemed to care. Chance, she reminded herself. There was always a chance for them.

If he could accept her baby.

Maybe Connie was right. Maybe if he fell in love and a child was part of the package, he would be happy about it, in spite of his past.

Thea checked over the Mother's Day fare she'd set up in Scott's parent's home one last time to reassure herself it was perfect. So far, their covert operation had come off without a hitch. The night before, Kendra had helped her assemble the food and decorations, deciding a big banner and balloons were inexpensive and easy. When Thea had arrived, the house was empty so she assumed the movie idea had worked like a charm. Thea had decorated and set out the food, plates and utensils.

Now that everything was ready, she had a few moments to catch her breath and look around. The elder Matthews lived in a sprawling ranch-style house not far from Scott's in a gated community. The living and dining rooms were situated on either side of the entryway that led to the huge kitchen with an island in the center. Thea browsed through the adjacent family room with its used brick fireplace and matching raised hearth that took up almost a whole wall.

Family pictures were everywhere, including some of Scott and his brother. She studied a photo collage on the wall and recognized Scott's formative years. There was one of him as a little boy playing T-ball, a grade school play, junior high, high school football, then him with an infant in his arms. It hit her that the pace of his formative years had suddenly increased at the speed of light. There was no picture parade of girlfriends like his brother had. He'd gone straight from high school football to fatherhood.

Before the knot in her stomach had a chance to tighten, she heard a car in the drive. Peeking out of the living room window, she saw doors on two vehicles open and the Matthews clan spilled out. Her gaze was drawn to Scott like a magnet to true north and her heart skipped in a way that was becoming familiar at the first sight of him.

His brother Mike bore a striking family resemblance. He was as tall as Scott, with the same dark hair and hunk quotient. But the family photos hadn't revealed a Mrs. Mike and she wondered about that. Kendra and Gail were both there with an older couple who must be their grandparents. Laughing and talking, the whole Matthews family walked up the brick sidewalk. Thea hurried into the kitchen. When everyone walked in, they stopped and stared—first at her, then at the banner.

Thea looked at Kendra and grinned. Together they said, "Surprise!"

Scott read the words on the hand-lettered sign— Happy Mother's Day, Grandma. Happy Mother's Day, Dad. With a pleased, yet puzzled expression on his face, he looked at his daughter. "What's all this?"

Kendra stood by the kitchen island and twisted her

fingers together. "You've been both mother and father to Gail and me, and Father's Day didn't seem like enough. I just wanted to do something special to say thanks."

The older woman hugged her granddaughter, then sniffled and wiped away a tear. "Now I know why you were so insistent about getting us out of the house to that dreadful movie. That business about starting new family traditions. And this is why you threw that fit about not wanting to go out to dinner afterward. All that drama about starving to death while waiting to get a table." She shook her head as she smiled fondly at the teen.

Kendra shrugged. "I didn't know what else to do when you suggested that new restaurant by the theaters. I worked my fingers to the bone on this."

"You certainly were a big help," Thea agreed wryly.

"Thanks." Kendra grinned at her. "Are you surprised?" she asked, looking from her father to her grandmother.

"Absolutely," they both said.

"So was I," said the older man, who was obviously Scott's father. Tall, silver-haired, distinguished, he was the image of what his son would look like as he aged.

And Thea realized how very much she would like to know Scott for a long time and watch him grow distinguished. But the thought scared her because she didn't trust the future.

Before she could process that information further, Scott met her gaze and smiled. "Kendra, this is obviously your gig. Maybe you should introduce everyone to Thea."

The teen nodded and cleared her throat. "Family, this is Thea Bell, from For Whom the Bell Toils catering. Thea, this is my family."

"Smart aleck," Scott said, shaking his head. He put his arms around his mother and father. "These are my parents—Betty and Tom."

The older woman was a short, slim brunette. Her brown eyes still sparkled with a suspicious brightness. "It's nice to meet you, dear."

"The pleasure is mine, Mrs. Matthews, Mr. Matthews."

"It's Betty and Tom," the older man said. He indicated the man beside him. "This is our youngest son Mike."

Scott's brother studied her openly. "I've heard a lot about you. It's nice to finally meet the woman giving my brother fits," he said, smiling.

She was dealing with the fact that he was every bit as good-looking as his older brother and it took several moments before his words sank in. "Fits?"

Scott looked uncomfortable. "Mike has a big mouth."

Betty glanced from one son to the other, her gaze finally settling on the youngest. "Michael what are you talking about?"

"Nothing, Mom. Call it payback for years of sibling oppression."

"I never picked on you," Scott said with over-the-top, self-righteous indignation.

"Okay." Mike's grin was full of the devil. "And because you're lying, I will revert to junior high mentality for just a moment. Scott likes Thea."

"I can see why," Tom said, studying her. "And we all know the way to a man's heart is through his stomach. Why do you think I married your mother?"

But the levity did nothing to disarm the glare Scott turned on his brother. "You just violated some serious sibling code. And, for the record, I never picked on you."

"You still pick on him, Dad," Gail said. "Hi, Thea."

She was glad to have the focus off her and Scott. But it was clear he'd talked to his brother about her. Was that good or bad?

"Hi, kiddo," Thea said. "How's UCLA?"

She beamed. "Way cool. Although finals are coming up fast."

Thea nodded and glanced at the Matthews clan. "It's nice to meet you all. Now it's time to get this celebration on the road. I've set all the food up in here." She indicated the hot trays on the kitchen island containing lasagna and stuffed shells. "Your backyard and patio are so beautiful, I decided to set up the picnic table out there."

Scott went to the window and looked out. "Wow." He glanced back at her. "It looks great. You did a terrific job."

His compliment pleased her more than a compliment usually did, proving that she was in a lot of trouble. "I'm glad you approve. Now everyone, the plates are here. Fill them up and I'll get drinks when you're all settled at the table."

"Of course you'll join us," Betty said.

"Thank you, no. I'm working," she explained.

"I don't know how Kendra roped you into this," the older woman said, "but I'm going to make an educated, instinctive guess that she's supposed to be helping."

"Yes, but she's part of the family and this is a family party. You all don't want a stranger intruding."

"You're not a stranger." Scott's mouth turned up at the corners.

The twinkle in his eyes told her he was thinking

about seeing her naked, which supported his statement. Thea's cheeks couldn't have been hotter if she'd been cooking over an open fire.

"I'm the caterer," she explained. "It's my job to be unobtrusive—to not be seen or heard."

"I thought that was kids," Mike Matthews said.

"No, Uncle Mike." Gail huffed out a breath. "Kids should be *seen* and not heard."

"Then how come you didn't get the memo?" Mike playfully grabbed her and rubbed his knuckles over the top of her head until she shrieked for mercy.

Betty Matthews stepped forward and handed Thea a plate. "You may be the caterer, but this is my house and no one goes hungry. Besides, you're too skinny."

Scott shrugged. "I think you just had your first example of what Mike and I learned many years ago."

"What's that?" Thea asked.

"Don't mess with Mom."

Thea smiled at the woman who'd taken back control of her kitchen, removing plastic from the salad, uncovering steaming dishes of food and directing traffic through her domain.

"Well, I tried," she said to Scott. The two of them were at the end of a line of Matthews family members filling their plates as they filed past the food. "Your mom is obviously happier running the show."

"She is now that food she didn't have to prepare is here and assembled," he said. He sniffed the fragrance of basil and garlic wafting through the air. He sighed dramatically. "You're amazing. I think I've died and gone to heaven."

"Not yet." Mike turned and looked at him. "But I can arrange it."

Thea laughed. "You remind me of my brother."

Mike looked offended. "Not exactly what a guy wants a pretty girl to say."

"Not so fast, little brother. I saw her first."

The tone got Thea's attention and when she looked at Scott, she wondered if he was angry. Did he think his brother was hitting on her? The idea that he might be jealous filled her with a sense of awe. She wasn't the sort of woman men fought over. And it certainly wasn't her intention to manipulate the two of them, but the fantasy of two such attractive men vying for her attention was so incredibly lovely. The rush of exuberance filled her with sheer happiness to be alive.

And for the first time since losing her husband, that thought wasn't followed by a flood of guilt.

"That was a test." Mike grinned. "And I found out what I wanted to know."

"I should have taken you out when I could have," Scott mumbled, flexing his wide shoulders as if they were tense.

When all the plates were full and everyone else was seated at the table beneath the patio cover, Scott pulled a chair up beside his own for Thea before the two of them sat down. Her heart stumbled at the masculine gesture that was just shy of possessive.

She dug into the food on her plate, realizing she was very hungry. Fortunately, the Matthews clan went into action, laughing, talking, teasing. This gave her a chance to observe them.

The mutual love, respect, and acceptance was evident in the good-natured banter and joking. They reminded her of her own family. She'd been raised in a similar environment and had always yearned to have that same kind of life. But fate had stepped in and robbed her of the chance.

"So, Thea, I understand you'll be catering Kendra's graduation party." Betty took a bite of garlic bread and closed her eyes for a moment as she chewed, an expression of sublime enjoyment suffusing her expression.

"That's right." She looked at the teenager. "In just a few weeks, she'll be the proud owner of a high school diploma."

"And it's about darn time," Scott said. "What took you so long, kidlet?"

The words, teasing though they were, twisted in Thea's chest. He was obviously happy to be almost finished with child-rearing and she'd barely begun. He was such a good father, with so much to offer. And that was when she pushed the thought away and ate as if this were her last meal.

When everyone declared that they couldn't eat another bite, Thea stood to clear the dishes and Kendra helped.

Gail joined them in the kitchen, resting her elbows on the island. "The food was great, Thea."

"I'm glad you liked it."

"The most important thing is that Grammy did. And Dad. Way to go, sis," Gail said. "Wish I'd thought of it."

"Thanks." Kendra flashed a grin over her shoulder as she loaded the dishwasher. Then she looked at Thea. "What about your mom? I'm sorry. I didn't even think. Was she okay with you doing this on Mother's Day?"

"My brother and sister and I took her and Dad out for brunch," she explained. "That's been our tradition for several years, which left me free this evening."

"We're glad you're free, too. If you were a mom, you wouldn't be," Gail said. A thoughtful expression settled on her pretty face. "How come you're not? Do you want children?"

"Yes."

"How do you know? How do you decide when it's right to have kids?" Kendra asked.

Thea knew the question was generated by her family history. Her father had never had the opportunity to choose when he wanted to *be* a father.

"I don't know about timing," she admitted. "But I do know that ever since I was a little girl, I've wanted to have a baby."

"So how come you don't?" Kendra asked.

Thea couldn't say anything to them about her dream nearly come true—not until she told Scott about the baby. When he walked through the sliding glass door connecting the kitchen to the patio, she knew she had to tell him soon.

"Hey, you guys," he said to his daughters. "I can't hold your grandmother back any longer. She's opening your gifts whether you're there or not."

"No," Kendra said. "I want to see her face."

"Me, too," her sister said as the two of them hurried back outside.

Scott came up behind her and slipped his arms around her waist. "I thought I'd never get you alone."

"So you lied?"

"How did you know?" he asked, chuckling into her ear.

"I thought you never lied."

"It's not a lie as much as a man's gotta do what a man's gotta do."

His breath stirred the hair around her face and raised tingles all over her body. How she wanted to lose herself in his arms.

But Scott must have felt her body tense because he turned her toward him. "Is something wrong?"

"No," she lied. Correction: a woman had to do what a woman had to do. And right now she didn't want to spoil his night.

His gaze skimmed her own and he shook his head. "I can see it in your eyes. What's going on?" He pointed a finger at her. "And don't tell me it's nothing."

"It can wait," she hedged. "This isn't the time."

"If you're upset about something, I'll make time. Spill it, lady. It's not good to keep things bottled up." She started to put him off again, but he silenced her with that same pointed finger over her lips. "Just so we're clear, I don't intend to let this drop until you've come clean."

Interesting choice of words. But now she really had no choice. As if she ever did. Twice she'd tried to tell him and both times he'd interrupted her with a kiss that scrambled her brain function. This was lousy timing, but there simply wasn't going to be a perfect time and place for this announcement. And one thing she'd learned about Scott—when he made up his mind, he wouldn't back off. Now that he'd insisted, she needed to just say it.

"I just have something to tell you."

"What?" He frowned as he studied her face. "Interest rates went sky-high? You're moving to Micronesia? Global warming ruined the world's garlic and herb crop?"

She shook her head and took a deep breath. "Mother's Day seems as appropriate a time as any to tell you I've always wanted to be a mother."

His hands stilled on her arms. "You have?"

"Yes. In fact, I'm going to have a baby in about six months."

Chapter Thirteen

Scott couldn't have been more shocked if she'd stripped naked and slugged him in the gut. He would have bet everything he owned that she hadn't been intimate with another man since her husband died. How could he have been so wrong? The bitterness of her betrayal slammed through him.

"So that's what you meant when you said you were okay. If you're already pregnant, I suppose that qualifies as birth control," he said, his throat tight. "Were you going to try to pass it off as mine?"

She took a step back, looking genuinely shocked. "Whatever you're thinking, you couldn't be more wrong."

"I'm thinking who's the father?"

"My husband."

"That would take a miracle."

"Exactly." She nodded. "A miracle of modern science. The magic of IVF."

"What?"

"In vitro fertilization."

"But your husband's been gone two years."

Thea leaned back against the sink and folded her arms over her chest. The smooth skin of her forehead puckered. From outside, sounds of laughter drifted in through the open window. At least his family was having a good time.

"When David was diagnosed with cancer," she finally said, "we were trying to have a baby. The oncologist told us that chemotherapy was the only chance to save his life, but it would make him sterile. It would be impossible for him to father the child we so desperately wanted. We were advised to freeze sperm."

"I see."

"When the treatment put him in remission, we didn't want to waste any time. We consulted a fertility specialist who guided us through IVF. He injected me daily with ovulation stimulants before my eggs were harvested and combined with his sperm in a petri dish."

"Then what?"

"The cells multiplied and divided. After that, three fertilized embryos were implanted and the rest were frozen. We thought we'd hit a home run first time at the plate. I was pregnant." Anguished sadness crept into her face. "Three months later, I had a miscarriage. We were crushed. Then we tried again, but the same thing happened. We were devastated. But there was more bad news. David's cancer came back."

Scott tried to wrap his mind around what she was telling him. She was pregnant. Her dead husband was the father. The words banged around inside him and he felt as if he were slipping into a black hole. At the same time he was angry that she looked so sad for another man. A man who'd lost his fight to live. What kind of bastard was he to be resentful because she'd loved the guy with everything she had?

"Scott, I promised my husband that I would do everything in my power to make sure a part of him went on."

"But it's been two years. Why now?"

"Lots of factors. I had no reason to believe the results would be any different this time, but time was the operative word. I'm thirty-four years old. Twenty-five percent of women under thirty-five achieve live births. After that, the rate drops with each year over thirty-five. Also, I had to make a decision about what to do with the frozen embryos. I couldn't give them to strangers or pull the plug and let them go. I had enough left for one more try and figured I had nothing to lose."

Maybe *she* had nothing to lose. But he felt as if he was losing everything. If only she'd said something…

Anger churned through him and settled in his gut like acid. "What I don't get is why you didn't tell me right away."

"I should have, I guess."

"You guess?" His voice rose as waves of what ifs washed over him. If only he'd known. If only he could have insulated himself. If he'd simply shut down his instantaneous attraction to her from day one. If he'd done any of the above, he wouldn't be fighting off the pain that threatened to pull him under now.

"After everything I'd been through, I didn't know if I could survive another miscarriage. Emotionally, I mean."

"What does that have to do with telling me the truth?"

"You make it sound like a deliberate lie."

"Isn't it?"

She shook her head as something—anger, irritation, fear—flashed through her dark eyes. "I'm not in the habit of blurting out my personal information to complete strangers."

"I'm not a stranger."

"You were at first. When you got to *not* be a stranger, the situation became awkward. How do you slide something like that into a conversation with a client? I make a mean egg roll. Oh, and by the way I'm pregnant? It wasn't any of your business. Besides, I'd made a promise to myself not to say anything to anyone until after I made it safely through the first trimester of my pregnancy."

"And are you? Through the first three months?"

His gaze dropped to her still flat stomach. He'd seen her naked, the feminine beauty of her soft curves, her full breasts. Not a single sign had alerted him to the fact that she was carrying a baby. But he hadn't been looking for signs. He'd been too busy savoring the feel of her and wondering how he'd gotten so lucky the day he'd come home and found Thea in his kitchen. He figured his bad karma was over. No one told him karma had a sick sense of humor.

"I completed the first trimester not long ago."

"Before we had sex the first time?" She flinched, then met his gaze and nodded. "At that point, I'd say it was definitely my business."

"I'd been trying to find the words to tell you, then you kissed me," she said, twisting her fingers together.

"You're blaming me for the fact that you didn't clue me in about something I had every right to know?"

"Of course not." Her eyes flashed again, and her lips pressed together for a moment. "I distinctly remember saying I had something to tell you. Your response was 'me first' and then you kissed me and I couldn't think about anything else."

"Oh, please. You think flattery is going to make this better?"

"It's not flattery. The truth is it felt good. I'd forgotten how good it felt to be in a man's arms. Your arms," she said, putting a finer point on the statement. "And making love. I simply couldn't think about anything else. It was wonderful to reaffirm that I'm still a woman. Not just a vessel for my child or a glorified science experiment. But a flesh and blood woman with wants, needs, passions. And to know that you wanted me. Do you have any idea how much that meant to me?"

He had a clue. What she said touched a nerve with him. "That still doesn't justify what you did. Or should I say didn't do."

"It's still something that's my personal information. I was trying to find a way to tell you, then you shared how adamantly opposed you are to having children. After that I knew there could never be anything between us and figured there was no reason to tell you."

"That's where you're wrong. There was a damn good reason. I don't sleep with someone I don't care about. So where does that leave me?" He saw the shadows in her eyes and couldn't find the will to care that he was being harsh. "All you had to do was be up front and everything would have been fine."

Scott realized there was more than one way to be trapped. He'd felt that as a young father, his choices taken away when he did the "right" thing. Then his wife had walked out leaving him alone and solely responsible for their two small children. Now he was torn between his powerful feelings for Thea and his desire not to be tied down again.

"I'm sorry, Scott. If there was something else I could say or do, I would. But there isn't. So take me out back and throttle me."

"I'm not in the habit of throttling women." He ran his fingers through his hair. "But for God's sake, Thea. I've been in the parenting trenches for twenty years. My kids are almost independent. To start all over—"

"I've heard that children keep you young," she said,

He stared at her and hated the hope he saw in her eyes. "Twice I was robbed of choices. After that, I did something to make sure I was completely in control." That was a laugh. Control was a pipe dream. "I had a vasectomy."

"Oh. That's what you meant when *you* said you were safe."

Her eyes widened and her mouth trembled before she caught her top lip between her teeth. That told him she understood how much he didn't want to be responsible for another child. But he couldn't help feeling he'd drop-kicked a kitten and the thought ticked him off. He hadn't done anything wrong.

"I can't believe this." He slammed his fist on the counter, ignoring the pain that vibrated up his arm and settled in his shoulder. "I finally connect with someone—with you—and now this."

"Don't feel like the Lone Ranger. I didn't expect to ever have strong feelings for another man. Yet here I am."

In spite of everything, pleasure shot through him at her admission, but he tried to ignore it. This was an impossible situation.

"Yeah, here we are. With a baby standing between us."

She tipped her head to the side as she studied him. Anger flashed through her eyes and mixed with the pain. "You know, Scott, I never expected to feel alive again and didn't care to. You were right. I've just been going through the motions. It never occurred to me that I would care for someone again. And it especially didn't cross my mind that someone I liked and respected would view a new life as a negative."

"Don't you dare make this my fault," he ground out.

"Nothing could be further from the truth. I'm just explaining that this child is the most important thing in the world to me. I lost two babies. The crushing pain of that taught me it's not just about having a child. I learned how desperately I wanted to be a mother."

"So what are we going to do?" he asked, frustration roiling through him.

"Under the circumstances, it might be easier if you found another caterer to do Kendra's party. I can recommend some good, reputable ones."

He shook his head and didn't want to think about why everything in him cried out against that suggestion. "Time is getting short. And besides, Kendra wanted you. The party is about her, not us."

"I agree. And there's no way I would do anything to hurt her, but I had to offer." She sighed. "And I understand if you want to back out of the house deal—"

"Why would I? To hurt you?" The thought never crossed his mind.

She lifted one shoulder. "I wouldn't blame you."

"No. That, at least, still feels right." In fact, it felt more right than it did before, reaffirming that he was going to control his life if it was the last thing he did.

"Okay." She nodded. "Then we'll get through everything the best we can. After that, we don't have to see each other again."

As Thea turned away to pack up her things, Scott felt as if she'd already left. He hated the thought of not seeing her, of not having her in his life. The emptiness hit him low and deep. He hadn't known he could feel so much so fast. Possibilities had dangled in front of him and now they were snatched just out of reach.

Maybe he was a selfish bastard, but he wanted time to think only about himself. Hadn't he earned it? His head said yes. The tightness in his chest told him something else.

Thea checked the heat beneath the chafing dish to make sure the flame wasn't high enough to dry out the lasagna. She'd set up the food for Kendra's party on the kitchen island and dinette. All the guests had moved through, filled their plates and then filed out the slider to the tables set up around the pool in the backyard. Now she was checking everything to make sure the remaining food would hold up to second helpings. Sometimes they were better than the first time around. Other times, not so much.

Kind of like her and Scott. Both of them were each other's seconds and they'd been a disaster. He'd been conspicuously absent today when she'd set up for the party. And tonight she'd managed to look extremely busy when he'd gotten his food. How could she have been so stupid as to think he might care enough about her that a package deal would be okay with him?

She thought about his vasectomy and wondered why she'd been so shocked that he'd taken the ultimate step to make absolutely certain he would have no more children. From the first moment she'd met him, he'd made no secret of the fact that his youngest child was almost on her own. He had mixed feelings about it but he couldn't keep her from growing up. He was moving on and making the best of it.

For the record, she was never listening to Connie again about hoping for something she knew in her heart wasn't going to happen.

From her vantage point in the kitchen, she surveyed the Matthews backyard. She'd messed up with Scott, but at least she'd done a good job for his daughter's party. The decorations looked great. They'd strung white lights in the trees and set up tables on the brick deck surrounding the pool. Centerpieces were mortarboards and balloons— the sky's the limit. Napkins for each place setting were rolled up and tied with a ribbon to look like a diploma.

Everyone seemed to be having a good time, she thought, glancing around at the group of relatives and friends. Thea recognized the Matthews clan. They'd all been very friendly tonight so she guessed Scott hadn't clued them in on anything. She thought about the first and last time she'd seen them. Pain rolled through her and she knew it would be hard from now on to celebrate Mother's Day without remembering how she'd had her heart broken for the second time.

As much as she tried not to, her gaze continually strayed to Scott. She'd caught him looking at her more than once. Every time, his mouth tightened and he looked angry as he immediately glanced away. She didn't blame him for any of this. It was all her fault. He was right. She should have said something. But she'd thought she was doing the right thing. After losing her babies, it had been beyond painful when people had asked how she was feeling. She'd had to put on a brave face and say over and over what had happened. This time, keeping her condition to herself had been every bit as painful—in a very different way.

Kendra walked inside with her empty plate. "Wow, that was really good. Is there anything left?"

"Everything. What can I get you?"

"Actually, nothing. I'm stuffed," the teen admitted. "I was just making an excuse to talk to you."

"You don't need an excuse. Why would you think that?"

"I don't know."

"Well I'm glad you did. I wanted to thank you for the graduation invitation. I wish I could have gone, but…" She shrugged, unable to find the words.

"That's okay. Thanks for the gift."

"You're welcome." Thea had sent a very feminine, cloth-covered photo album that tied with a ribbon so that Kendra could keep memories of this time. But as she studied the girl, she realized something was bothering her. "What's wrong, sweetie?"

She lifted one shoulder. "It's just that everything feels different."

"With your dad?" Thea asked. "Did something happen?"

Kendra shook her head. "No. At least not between dad and me. But he's been weird."

"Weird how?" It was nothing more than a stall tactic.

"Grumpy. Testy. Crabby."

"Sounds like three of the Seven Dwarfs from the dark side," Thea commented.

Kendra laughed. "He's like he used to be. Only worse."

"Like he used to be?"

"Yeah. Before he met you."

"He changed?" Thea asked, hating that she couldn't stop the tiny little glow inside her.

"Yeah. For a while there he was happy. And cool. And he listened. Now he's not happy. Ever since that Mother's Day party."

"Oh."

"I was just wondering. Maybe that idea wasn't so hot. Did I do something?" she asked, clearly confused and upset.

"No, of course not." Thea touched the girl's arm, feeling the need to connect and make her understand.

"How can you be so sure?"

"Because it's me he's angry at."

The girl's eyes grew wide. "That's why he got so irritated when I wanted to give you an invitation to my graduation."

It warmed her heart that this young woman she'd grown fond of had wanted her to be a part of her commencement day, enough to send the invitation against her father's wishes. She also understood Scott's negative reaction, but his daughter didn't.

Kendra nodded. "Dad went ballistic and said I couldn't invite the whole universe."

Thea wasn't that big with child yet. "Who else did you want there?"

"My mom." Shadows lurked in her eyes. "He was mad, but I sent it anyway. It came back stamped Not At This Address."

"I'm sorry," she said, squeezing the girl's forearm reassuringly. She was even sorrier she hadn't attended the ceremony, even though Scott would have been annoyed. She'd let this girl down and that bothered her a lot.

One shoulder lifted in a careless shrug. "It's okay."

"No, it's not. And I think it's unconscionable the way that woman treats her children." Then rational thought returned. "I'm sorry. I should keep my opinion of your mother to myself."

Surprisingly, Kendra didn't look upset. "No. I think she's pretty lame, too. But I'm sorry Dad wouldn't let you come to the ceremony. What happened between you two? I thought he kind of liked you. And you liked him, too."

Thea wasn't going to tell this young woman that her father was giving up on a promising relationship because of the baby Thea carried. It would be too easy for Kendra to go to the bad place where she blamed herself for his not wanting more children. The issue was complicated and Scott should be the one to explain his feelings.

"I think that's something you should ask your father," she gently suggested.

"But he won't tell me. He'll just pat me on the head and tell me not to worry about it."

"That's his prerogative."

"But it's not fair. He butts into my life and it's okay because he's my dad. But it's not okay to know what's bothering him?"

"He doesn't want you to be concerned." His single-minded determination to protect his children was one of the things Thea liked best about him. That and his outstanding butt, she thought a little sadly.

"He wants me to be responsible. He wants me to be a grown-up. It would help if he started treating me that way." Kendra looked confused and angry—and so much like her father that Thea's heart ached.

"He has mixed feelings about you growing up," Thea said, willing her to understand.

"No kidding. That's why I asked you. You've never sugarcoated anything for me. You've always been straight even when it wasn't something I wanted to hear."

Except this was different. It concerned hang-ups of Scott's that Thea wasn't at liberty to be straight about. But she felt she couldn't hang the teen out to dry completely.

"I can't speak for your father—"

Kendra cocked her hip and jammed her fist on it. "Please don't shut me down, Thea."

"You didn't let me finish," she pointed out. "I can't speak for him, but I can tell you how I feel. He's a wonderful man. He's kind, considerate, conscientious—"

"And hot?"

"Hard-working," she went on, ignoring the interruption. "He's a fabulous father."

"And you think he's really hot, right?"

"He's reliable and caring."

"Okay," Kendra said rolling her eyes. "I've had about all the grown-up treatment I can stand. Do you or do you not think my dad is the hottest thing since green Tabasco sauce?"

Thea laughed. "Okay. You win. I think your dad is a very nice-looking man."

Kendra shook her head. "Better, but no cigar. So you like him?"

"Yes."

"Then what's the problem?" she said, throwing up her hands.

"You're going to have to ask him that question."

The girl tapped her lip. "Then I have to assume you wouldn't kick him out of bed."

"What?" Thea's cheeks turned hot and it wasn't because the chafing dish flame was too high. Did this teenager know she'd slept with her father?

"Translation: you admitted you like my dad so that means he dumped you."

"No one dumped anyone." One had to be in a relationship for that to happen. She and Scott had sort of eased into something neither of them wanted to label and then they'd had mind-blowing sex. She didn't know what to call it.

"Then you guys still have a chance?"

"You're relentless," Thea said, shaking her head.

"Dad says determination is a good quality in a grown-up."

Like father, like daughter, she thought. He was the one who had refused to take no for an answer. If he had, neither of them would be in this mess now.

"Not being nosy is another admirable quality in an adult."

Kendra assumed a pathetic expression—big, wide eyes and semi-pouting mouth. "C'mon, Thea. Tell me something. I think I have a right to know. I liked you and my dad together. It made me feel better that he wouldn't be alone when I go away to school."

Hah. Wasn't that ironic. And Thea couldn't tell her that alone is exactly what Scott wanted. She wouldn't even tell her about being pregnant. It was the clue Kendra needed to put two and two together, but she might add it up to five. Scott needed to be the one to tell her and explain his feelings. He already blamed Thea for this lousy situation; and she'd accept a good portion of the responsibility. But she didn't want his daughter to jump to wrong conclusions because of anything she said. Still, she felt compelled to give Kendra something.

She sighed. "All I can tell you is that your father and I have something standing between us. And before you ask, there's no way for us to compromise on it."

"But if someone bends—"

Thea shook her head. "Ask him to explain."

"Why are all men dorks?" the girl asked, then heaved a big gusty sigh.

"Not all of them are. And when you meet a man who rings your chimes, I guarantee you won't think he's a dork."

"I'm never falling in love."

"Like I believe that." Thea laughed. "Now go back to your party. It's almost time for cake. And Connie worked long and hard on it."

"Okay." But the teen hesitated. "Can I call you? I mean, if there's anything I need to talk over, when I get to UCLA?"

Impulsively, Thea hugged her. "You can call me any time, sweetie. I sincerely mean that."

"Thanks." Then she walked outside and joined a group of teenage girls at a table under the trees.

Tears filled Thea's eyes as her gaze automatically went to Scott. A profound, aching sadness filled her as she stared at his handsome profile, smiling at something his brother said. Soon the party would be over and their only connection would be their respective escrows. When they closed, any link to him would be history.

If, as the saying went, timing was everything, then she had nothing. She'd been lucky enough to meet another wonderful man and she found it unbelievably tragic that there was no way to resolve their differences.

She'd worked so hard to keep from falling in love with Scott because deep down she'd known her heart would get broken.

And this was one time she hated being right.

Chapter Fourteen

The day after Kendra's party, Scott opened his door to the last person in the world he expected to see. The sight of Thea sent a jolt of joy arcing through him, followed almost instantly by a shaft of pain.

"Scott." She backed up a step, obviously surprised to see him. "I'm sorry. I-I...Kendra said you weren't home," she finished lamely. Nervously, she tucked a strand of hair behind her ear.

So that was why his daughter had looked so funny after answering the phone and out of the blue said she was going to the mall. She was playing matchmaker. "Sorry. I still live here until escrow closes."

He hadn't meant to sound so abrasive. But it was hard to concentrate when his brain was busy memorizing the way the sun picked out the red in her brown hair and made it flash and sparkle with even the slightest movement.

She was staring at him, too. "I don't mean to bother

you. But last night I left some serving dishes and a few other things after the party. I stopped by to pick them up." She met his gaze, then half turned away. "But it's all right. I can do it another time."

He shook his head. "Now's fine."

Even though it hurt to look at her. Deep inside, where no woman had ever touched him before, he ached. Watching her throughout the party last night had been a mixture of pleasure and pain. Pleasure because just looking at her did that to him. And pain because he couldn't have her, not under the circumstances.

When she'd left last night, it was as if some light inside him sputtered and went out. He figured that was the last time he would see her. And he was resigned to that. The lie was bitter inside him, although he would make it the truth if it was the last thing he ever did. But at this very moment, he couldn't make himself send her away.

"Come in."

"Thanks. Kendra said she stacked the things on the island in the kitchen. I'll just get them and be out of your hair."

Just because she walked out of his house didn't mean she would be out of his hair. Not as long as he couldn't stop thinking about her.

He sighed as he followed her to the back of the house. It took every ounce of his self-control to keep from pulling her against him and kissing her until they were both breathless and wanting.

In the kitchen, he spotted her stuff on the island, just as she'd said. He cleared his throat and, if there was a God in heaven, his voice would be normal, or at the very least, neutral.

"Yeah. Here it is," he said.

She inspected the sizable stack of serving dishes, warming trays and assorted spoons and linens. "It looks like everything is here."

When she started to grab the collection, he put his hand on her bare arm to stop her. Warmth from her skin zinged through him, leaving sparks that threatened to reignite that light inside him.

He took his hand away and forced himself to ignore the tingle that wouldn't stop. "I'll take that out for you."

"Thanks, but that's not necessary. It's bulky but not heavy. I can handle it."

"You're pregnant," he said simply. But there was nothing simple about those two words. They changed everything and turned his world upside down.

"Having a baby, true. But I'm not handicapped. I carry things all the time."

"Maybe you shouldn't. Why didn't you send Connie to pick this up?"

"Because I can handle it."

"For someone who was so cautious she wouldn't even talk about her condition, this attitude seems a tad cavalier."

The angry words told him he hadn't achieved neutrality toward her yet.

A muscle moved in her jaw as her eyes flashed. "Okay. If you're going to keep up the martyr routine and be snarky, there's no reason I should soft-pedal anything. I didn't send Connie to pick up these things because she's pretty angry with you and I couldn't guarantee your safety."

He was the one who'd been kept in the dark from day one, he thought. Although her "martyr routine" crack cut deep.

"What the heck did I do?" he asked.

"You hurt me."

"*I* hurt *you?*" he said. "Excuse me, but weren't you the one withholding pertinent information?"

"Think back, Scott. And be honest with yourself. I tried to keep distance between us. I tried to get you to back off. But you and your pesky determination wore me down."

"You knew from day one how I felt about being finished with raising children. All you had to say was, 'I'm pregnant.'"

"I hardly knew you from a rock," she snapped. "I'm not in the habit of revealing intimate details of my life to any Tom, Dick or Harry on the street."

"You were in my house."

"Don't split hairs. You were a client. That didn't entitle you to my personal, private information."

He put his hands on his hips as he stared at her. "Has your life always been this top secret?"

"As a matter of fact, no. I used to be much more open. But that changed when I opened my big mouth to people I thought were my friends. I found out you can't trust anyone."

He had a bad feeling about what had put the wary, wounded look in her eyes. Maybe she wouldn't answer, but he decided to ask anyway. "What happened?"

Her eyes glowed with anger. "It was right after David was diagnosed with cancer. He had a lot of paid time off that he could take for treatment and wanted to keep his condition just between the two of us."

"What happened?"

"I decided that for him to successfully fight the disease, he needed the support of everyone around him, including his co-workers."

"And?" This was like pulling teeth.

"And I found out the hard way that my husband's instincts were right. He was one of two candidates in line for a promotion with more benefits. The other guy went to his boss and revealed David's condition. He was advanced. David was put on administrative leave—sick leave, they said. And claimed it was in his best interests so he could concentrate on getting well. But we had to pick up the cost to keep our medical insurance in force. Administration wanted to unload deadweight." She laughed harshly. "No pun intended."

"That doesn't seem right. Surely you had some recourse?"

Her mouth tightened for a moment before she said, "I wanted to fight it, but David didn't have the stamina to battle on two fronts. And his health was the most important fight. That was when I started catering on the side to earn extra money. I was an office manager by day. But we'd opted to take our medical benefits through David's job and after his diagnosis, he had a pre-existing condition and no insurance company would touch him. So they got away with it."

He ran his fingers through his hair. "That's rough."

"It was a nightmare. A painful lesson. But it taught me to play my cards close to the vest."

"Yeah. But, you and I—this was an entirely different situation."

"Oh? I was here for a catering job. How was I to know you wouldn't say pregnant caterers need not apply?"

"Now *you're* splitting hairs. Besides, pretty soon you won't be able to hide your condition."

"I wasn't hiding anything. And like I said, I tried to get you to back off, but you wouldn't. I didn't set out to make you fall for me. And I certainly didn't intend to—" She brushed the back of her hand across her cheek. "Oh, never mind. This is pointless."

"No. You didn't intend to what?"

Her eyes blazed when she met his gaze. But mixed in with the sparks were tears. "I didn't intend to fall for anyone. My goal is to bring a healthy baby into this world and raise him or her by myself to be the best human being possible. This child is a part of David. After the way I betrayed him, the least I can do is make sure his DNA will go on."

"Are you still in love with him?"

Scott wasn't sure what made him ask. But suddenly it was damned important for him to know.

Her chin lifted just a fraction and the sparks in her eyes burned out, leaving only the tears. "I'll always love David."

She looked at the stack of things beside her as she rubbed a knuckle beneath her nose. "You know, suddenly warming trays and serving dishes aren't so important. Since we're closing escrow soon, just leave them for me when you move out."

She slid him a weak smile, then walked past him and out the front door.

Scott felt as if he'd been flattened by a three-hundred-pound linebacker. She still loved her husband?

"This bites," he snapped.

He wanted to hit something. The pain might take the edge off what he felt inside.

And he had to admit Thea was right. He'd noticed her putting distance between them. And he'd planned to play it her way until his brother talked him into giving it one more try.

"Remind me to thank Mike," he said to the empty room.

He was angry at Thea. Angry at his brother. But mostly, he was furious with himself because he still wanted her.

And he didn't know how to make it stop.

Thea walked up the plant- and shrub-lined sidewalk to the escrow company. When the loan officer had called to set the time for signing papers, Thea had made sure Scott was already scheduled in the morning before settling on her own last appointment of the day.

As much as she ached to see him, just to catch a glimpse of him, it was best that she didn't. He was angry and she couldn't really blame him. It was all her fault—wrong thing, right reason. Lousy result. She had to move on with her life. She'd done it before, after David's death. She could do it again.

After muscling open the heavy glass-and-chrome door, she walked into the lobby. Searching the building's directory there, she found the suite number and then took the elevator to the third floor. When the doors whispered open, she stepped out into the reception area. It should have been empty. It wasn't. Scott was there, dwarfing one of the standard waiting room chairs.

Her body betrayed her good intentions to move on without him. Her traitorous heart hammered almost painfully, making it difficult to draw in air. On legs that felt about as sturdy as limp noodles, she moved farther into the room.

He looked up. For a split second, she'd swear he was glad to see her. Then his mask of cool indifference slipped into place. It was the expression he'd worn the day after the party, two weeks ago, when she'd told him why she didn't share her personal information. She hadn't seen or heard from him since.

"Hi," she said.

He stood. "Hi."

Then she got a bad feeling. "I thought you were signing papers this morning. Is there a problem?"

Translation: had he changed his mind about the real estate deal? God knows she'd had second thoughts about living in the house that would forever hold his essence. In a weird way, that thought had actually brought her comfort. Probably because she was completely pathetic.

"No problem. Except I had to reschedule my appointment." He lifted one broad shoulder in a careless shrug. "A crisis at work."

At least he didn't think she'd scheduled her appointment in order to manipulate him somehow. "I hope it was nothing serious."

She meant that. Really she did. But it was difficult to be completely sincere. Not when the crisis had allowed her one more chance to memorize the laugh lines around his eyes, the mesmerizing blue there, and his strong, square jaw. The irony of the situation didn't escape her. They were buying each other's homes because they were at different places in their lives. And she had that to thank for this opportunity to see him one last time.

But the differences were also what stood between them.

"Nothing serious," he said absently, not looking away. "How are you?"

"Fine."

"And the baby?" His gaze dropped to her abdomen.

Her body was beginning to change and her clothes were getting a little snug. Her tummy was rounding nicely and all was as it should be, her doctor told her.

Everything was fine except for her heart. It would bear the scars of knowing Scott forever. But if he made love to her now, he'd notice her belly and know about the baby. The thought put a catch in her breathing at the same time it made her profoundly sad. A time that should have been perfectly joyful was marred by things that couldn't be changed.

"The baby's fine." She slid her purse strap higher on her shoulder. "My last ultrasound was normal and showed everything looks good."

"Did you find out the sex of the baby?"

She shook her head. "I want to be surprised."

"Are you hoping for a boy? To carry on David's name?"

How like a man to think of that. "It never occurred to me. I guess because girls are raised knowing their last name will change when they marry. But this child will carry David's DNA whether it's a girl or a boy. And that's all I care about."

He frowned and a muscle in his jaw jerked. "You look tired. Are you sure you're all right?"

"Fine," she said, with a snap in her voice that she couldn't suppress.

His rejection of her and the baby had absolved him of the right to be concerned about her. His being sweet and caring and tender was frustrating and just made everything harder.

"How's Kendra?" she asked, to change the subject.

"I haven't seen much of her. She's been shopping and getting ready to move down to school. There's a program for incoming freshmen to help them acclimate and get the most out of the college experience. It was her idea to do that and I agree it's a smart move."

If she'd just met him, she might have thought he was

trying to get rid of his daughter. But she knew him too well now. He only wanted what was best for his child, like any loving parent.

The last time Thea had seen Kendra was the night of the graduation party. She recalled the girl asking questions about their relationship and wondered if she'd quizzed him yet. If not, Thea should warn him so he could spin it whatever way he wanted.

"There's something you should know—"

"I hate when someone says that. The 'something' is never good."

She smiled and marveled that he could make her do that, what with all the pain bottled up inside her. "I didn't mean to be overly dramatic. It's just that I talked to Kendra the night of the party."

"And?"

"She asked about you and me." Thea couldn't quite meet his gaze. Her own settled on a spot just below his jaw, a place she'd very much enjoyed kissing.

"What did you tell her?" he asked sharply.

"Not much. I suggested she ask you."

"She hasn't said anything. What does 'not much' mean? She didn't even know there was a you and me."

"That's where you're wrong. She noticed. And she especially didn't miss the tension between us the night of the party."

"So what did you tell her?" Speaking of tension, his jaw tightened noticeably.

"I just said you were angry with me."

The last time she'd seen him, Thea had forgotten to warn him about this. Not surprising since she'd had a lot on her mind. Actually not a *lot*. Just Scott. But he felt like everything.

"Did you tell her you're pregnant?" he said, frowning.

"No. I thought it best that you explain."

He ran his fingers through his hair. "Swell."

It was on the tip of her tongue to say she was sorry, but Thea suppressed the words. Enough apologizing, already. She hadn't set out to hurt anyone. She'd tried to be true to herself and her child. If she had it to do over, she would do things differently. Hindsight was twenty-twenty. But she could have given Kendra an earful and didn't.

She put her hands on her hips. "Look, Scott, she asked and I had to tell her something. She's smart as a whip and noticed things changed between you and me after Mother's Day." How ironic was that? "She was afraid it was her fault somehow and I wouldn't let her think that. I told her there's something standing between us and there's no way to compromise."

"Hmm." His comment was just shy of a grunt.

Not especially helpful communication. "I didn't think it was fair to you that I explain your feelings to her. She's just gone through an insecure time and I didn't want to make it worse."

Thea stared at him, wondering how it was possible to be so angry with this man and so in love with him at the same time. The realization stunned her. She'd believed love would never again be in the cards for her. Yet it had happened. But no way would she admit as much to him. What was the point?

The door to the back offices opened and a plump blond woman stood in the doorway. "Ms. Bell?"

Thea looked at her. "Yes?"

"I can help you now."

No you can't, she thought. The woman had done the paperwork to make the rift between she and Scott official. He was condo; she was single-family home.

"Single" being the operative word. She glanced at Scott and the pain inside her expanded like a parachute after the rip cord had been pulled. It had been devastating to lose her husband to a disease she had no control over. And while he'd battled to survive, everyone had said where there was life, there was hope. She'd learned it was a lie. Scott was full of life, with so much to offer, and she had so much love to give. But it was never to be.

She met his gaze and hoped her own didn't betray what she was feeling. "I can wait to move into the house until after Kendra leaves for school."

He nodded. "Thanks. I appreciate that."

"I'm ready," she said to the escrow officer. She looked at Scott again feeling anything but ready—this was goodbye. And she couldn't bring herself to say it. "Good luck, Scott."

Then she turned away and followed the stranger past the point of no return. It was time to focus on her new home and getting it ready for her new baby. Forgetting the man who haunted every room wouldn't be easy, but she would do it.

She'd learned once that life is risky and love was the biggest risk of all. She'd just lost again.

Chapter Fifteen

Shaking his head, Scott surveyed Kendra's room. This time, the chaos wasn't her fault. Moving boxes designated for his town house were stacked against the wall. She had suitcases, several backpacks and a duffel filled with the personal stuff and school supplies that she was taking to her dorm room. All in all, the place didn't look much different from its normal disastrous state. Except this time, *he* was different. He knew she was taking the clutter and confusion with her to college, and a sinkhole of loneliness opened up inside him.

Kendra walked in and stuffed a brush into the side of her backpack. "I'm starting to freak about forgetting something."

Gail stood in the doorway. "It's not Timbuktu. It's UCLA. If you forget anything, I guarantee you can find a store that carries it."

Scott settled his arm across her shoulders and forced himself not to grab her to him and squeeze her tight.

He didn't because it's what he wanted to do to Kendra, to hang on and never let her leave home. But the reality was, they were all leaving this house.

Movers were scheduled to arrive tomorrow to take their belongings to Thea's town house. His now. They'd choreographed moving day carefully, both of them loading up at the same time, then the trucks passing like ships in the night. As always, thoughts of Thea sent a shaft of pain-wrapped regret slicing through him and he wondered if it would ever get better.

"What do you guys want to do about dinner?" he asked. "How about I take you to L'Italiano's. They have your favorite bread and that ravioli with the tomato cream sauce."

The girls looked at each other for a moment, then shook their heads. How did they do that silent communication thing? he wondered.

"I want to stay here," Kendra said, settling her duffel beside the suitcase at his feet. "It's my last night in this house."

"Mine, too," Gail echoed. "Although I don't think I feel it as much as Ken because I've been away for a couple years now."

"Then what about a pizza?" he said.

They looked at each other again and nodded. "That sounds good." Gail leaned her head against his shoulder.

His heart squeezed tight as he hugged her close for a moment, then dropped his arm. "I'll go call."

"Get it from Vincenzo's," Gail suggested. "It's my favorite."

"Mine, too," her sister echoed. "I think they deliver here so much, the driver could find his way blindfolded."

"Yeah," Gail said. "I've missed it."

"I'm going to miss it, too. And this house," Kendra said, a wistful expression on her face as she glanced around her room.

Gail sighed. "I keep telling myself change is part of being a grown-up. But myself answers back that I don't have to like it."

"Are you guys upset that I sold the house?" Scott asked.

He'd thought Kendra had come to terms with it after that first negative reaction. And the girls had seemed genuinely happy that Thea was buying the place. They approved of turning their house over to someone who would take good care of it. He'd tried to tell them it was business. But now that it was real, they were all feeling pretty darn personal about the change.

Kendra looked at him, her blue eyes shadowed. "We grew up here. All of my memories, good and bad, are here."

Gail met his gaze. "We moved here after Mom left. I've always wanted to ask you—" She caught her bottom lip between her teeth.

"What is it, honey? You can ask me anything."

"Well, I'm about the age now that you were when I was born. I guess I've been thinking about this since Ken went through that thing about you not wanting her. At school, I go to classes, hang out with my friends, do pretty much what I want. But you never got a chance to do that."

"So what's your question?"

"Do you have any regrets that I was born? Because of all you missed?"

"Never." He slung his arm around her again and this time, he did hug her close for several moments. "The two of you are the best thing that ever happened to me."

"But if Mom hadn't gotten pregnant with me, you'd have been able to go away to college. You didn't get to do a lot of things."

"I got to do other things, more important things. Like being a father to the two most terrific kids in the world." He rubbed his knuckles across the top of her head until she giggled and begged for mercy. Spinning away from him, she flopped on the bed beside her sister.

He crossed his arms over his chest as he leaned against the door frame. "But I will admit that I wonder sometimes what it would have been like to be ready for the experience of fatherhood."

Thea was responsible for that. She wanted it so much and had waited so long, he couldn't help thinking about what that would feel like. She had made him look at a lot of things differently.

He looked at his girls. "I love you guys and I wouldn't trade the two of you for anything."

"Speaking of love," Kendra said, a glint in her eyes, "what happened between you and Thea?"

Uh-oh. Thea had warned him this question might come up. How did he explain his feelings to them? The last thing he wanted was for them to feel insecure about their place in his heart.

"It's complicated," he finally said.

"Is it anything we did?" Kendra asked, glancing at her sister.

"Why would you think that?"

She shrugged. "I don't know. Maybe because of Mom. If it hadn't been for us, she might still be around. Maybe we chase women out of your life."

Residual anger and resentment churned through him, aimed at the woman who'd made his children blame themselves for her actions. He walked over to the bed and sat down between them, taking each of their hands in his.

"Okay, you two. Here's the deal. Straight, no bull. The reason your mother walked away from us had nothing to do with you. It was all about her and her selfish needs. It's as simple as that."

Kendra still looked unsure. "And what about Thea?"

How did he answer that? Kendra had brought her into his life. In spite of how it turned out, he couldn't regret knowing her. She was probably the most unselfish person he'd ever known. "She's one of a kind."

Gail snorted. "And that tells us exactly nothing. Do you like her? Are you dating? And what about—"

The doorbell rang and Scott was grateful. His eldest had a habit of blurting out personal questions, and he had a bad feeling he knew what she'd been about to say. He'd been saved by the bell and he couldn't quite suppress the hope that it was Thea Bell.

"I'll get it," he volunteered.

He started out of the room and glanced back at his girls. The sparkle was back in their eyes, just as it should be, and he went downstairs with a lighter heart.

He opened the door and found his brother on the porch. "Mike. What are you doing here?"

"I thought you might need some help with the move."

Scott didn't buy it. "You know this is Kendra's last night home and you came over to see her off."

"I'm that transparent?"

"Like plastic wrap," he said automatically.

He winced when he remembered Thea saying that to him. How long before he stopped thinking about her? Repeating her words? Seeing her face? Dreaming about her? Hoping she'd come to see him one last time to change his mind?

"Can I come in?"

"Yeah." Scott stepped back and pulled the door wide.

"I'm going to help myself to a beer."

"Get one for me."

When they were in the family room, long necks in hand, Mike looked at him. "I didn't just come to see Ken off."

"No?"

"I wanted to talk to you."

"About what?"

"Something's wrong, bro." He held up his hand when Scott started to protest. "Can it. You haven't been yourself since Mother's Day. Before you deny it, you should know the folks have noticed, too. Mom thinks it has something to do with Thea."

Scott thought about telling his brother to take a flying leap. But the truth was, he needed to talk about this. Maybe if he did, he could get her out of his mind.

"She's going to have a baby, Mike."

Unfortunately when he said that, his brother happened to be taking a drink. He choked for several moments. Finally he said, "I know it's not yours."

Scott shook his head. "It's her husband's."

"I thought she was a widow."

"She had in vitro fertilization, a promise she made to him before he died."

Mike blew out a long breath. "That would make a man stop and think."

"And this is me we're talking about." Scott shook his head. "My youngest is on her way to independence practically as we speak. To start again with night feedings, walking the floor, worrying. That's the hardest. Worrying about every little thing that could go wrong with that tiny human being who's looking to you for everything."

His brother stared at him. "It occurs to me that not once did you say you don't care about her."

"It doesn't matter—"

"That's where you're wrong, big brother. Caring is everything."

"But the baby stuff. Been there, done that. I don't want to do it again."

"With Thea, you wouldn't be alone this time."

"I wasn't alone the first time."

"Yes, you were. And I don't mean just after she left you." Mike leaned forward and rested his elbows on his knees, his beer in his hands. "Even when you were married, she wasn't ever really there for you. And she didn't care. If she did, she'd still be here."

"And your point?" Scott asked angrily.

"Thea's different."

"You hardly know her. How the heck can you decide that?"

"Actions speak louder than words. Your wife declared her undying love right up until she walked out. Thea loves so much, she moved heaven and earth to have her dead husband's child."

"I think she's still in love with him," Scott admitted. It was the first time he'd voiced that out loud. He wasn't sure if he felt relieved or not.

A gleam stole into his brother's gaze. "So that's what your problem is."

"What are you talking about?"

"You're looking for an excuse to turn your back because you might not measure up. She might reject you."

Scott snorted even as he felt the words strike a chord. "Stick to numbers, Mike. It's what you're good at."

"It doesn't take a psych degree to see you got the shaft real bad, bro. Even a spreadsheet guy like me can see you don't want to put yourself on the line and risk a repeat. But I saw the way she looked at you."

"How was that?" Scott kicked himself for asking, but couldn't stop the words.

"Her face lit up whenever she laid eyes on you. She's different, Scott," he said again. "And if you let her get away, you're an idiot."

Scott had one of those moments of absolute crystal clarity. Thea was loyal and loving and beautiful and smart. She was everything he'd ever wanted. And he was an idiot for building barriers to keep it from working between them.

He was in love with Thea Bell.

Scott felt one corner of his mouth curve up. "How the heck did an emotional train wreck like you figure all this out?"

"I'm the sensitive sort."

"Mom told you, didn't she?"

Mike grinned. "She thought the information would be better received if delivered man-to-man by someone closer to your age. She also said I might learn something."

"If you were smart enough, you'd have already learned from the two of them long before this."

"Right back at you," Mike said.

"Mom and Dad are the best," Scott pointed out, ignoring his brother's jab.

Mike didn't pretend to misunderstand. "Yeah. The folks are pretty lucky. I'd give a lot to find what they've got. I envy you, bro."

"Why?"

"A woman like Thea to care about. The chance to raise a child with her. Face it, Scott. You're a family kind of guy."

Mike was right. Damn it. Scott should have figured it out himself. He would have if his emotional baggage hadn't been stacked so high he couldn't see over it. He hoped his brother wasn't premature in patting him on the back. Scott knew it was entirely possible he'd blown the best thing that had ever happened to him.

He'd used the baby to push Thea away because it hurt when someone you cared about walked out. He'd successfully avoided caring too much until Thea somehow managed to infiltrate his heart.

The truth was family meant everything to him. It was how he'd grown up; it was how he'd raised his girls. He liked being a family man. He was good at it, if he did say so himself. Thea had a family in need of a man. And he was the right man for the job.

All he had to do was convince her of that.

Thea put a box filled with kitchen paraphernalia on her new island, then brushed the sweat off her forehead with the back of her hand.

"As God is my witness," she said to the room that looked like it threw up, "I vow two things. I'm never moving again. And if I buy a new kitchen gadget, I will throw an old one away."

She had entirely too much stuff. Thank goodness for all the cupboards she had now. Maybe she would renegotiate with God about throwing things away—if she ever forgave Him. It wasn't entirely His fault, but somewhere between running the world and being all-powerful, He could have worked a little miracle on her behalf with the former owner of this house.

But when she felt a little bubble move across her abdomen, she was reminded that her baby was a living miracle. "And I guess there's only one to a customer. Anything more would be greedy."

Besides, self-pity was a waste of energy. She'd been blessed, even though Scott didn't want her and the baby. It was his loss. Along with her son or daughter, she was going to have a good life in this house.

She looked around. The movers had left several hours before. After delivering all of her furniture, she realized the family room was still empty. A trip to a home-furnishing store was in her near future. And whatever she bought would need Scotchgarding. Not unlike the way her heart needed Scott-guarding.

"And procrastinating will not get the rest of the stuff out of my car."

She walked through the living and dining rooms, which were marginally more organized, but only because there were fewer things than in the kitchen. After walking out the front door, she followed the L-shaped walkway to where she'd backed her SUV in the driveway. With the back seat down, she'd been able to fill the car with the remainder of her things. The last minute stuff, like cleaning supplies and vacuum. She'd cleaned as the movers worked so Scott wouldn't have to worry about it.

Although it would have served him right if she'd left the dust bunnies and let them party hearty in every corner of the place. She knew she couldn't keep up this high level of anger and irritation toward him indefinitely. But she planned to maintain it for as long as possible. Because she knew from past experience when that was gone, she would be inundated by the pain.

When she rounded the garage, she stopped so fast her sneakers would have squeaked if she'd been standing on anything but cement. Speak of the devil.

"Scott," she said.

"Hi, Thea." He peeked into the back of her car. "That's quite a load."

"Yeah. I've got a million things to do. But you know how that is, what with moving into my place."

"Yeah." He had a weird expression on his face as if he'd eaten bad seafood.

"Is something wrong?"

"You could say that."

"But the condo passed inspection with flying colors. Everything was okay when I left."

"It's still fine."

She walked closer. The nearer she got to his tall, attractive self, the harder her heart pounded. "Then I don't understand. Are you having buyer's remorse? Because escrow is closed. You've taken title. There's no going back—"

He held up his hand. "No second thoughts. Not about buying the condo."

"Then what are you doing here?"

"I'm having second thoughts about you."

She couldn't believe she'd heard him right. But her heart kicked into high gear anyway. "What kind of thoughts?"

He ran his fingers through his hair. "Mike says I'm an idiot."

"You'll get no argument from me." She covered her mouth with her hand. "Sorry. Just popped out," she mumbled.

His expression turned sheepish. "I suppose I deserve that."

"No. What you deserve is a good swift kick in the caboose."

"Okay. I deserve that, too. I just didn't know what I had until it was gone."

Her gaze narrowed on him. "If you're talking about me, you never had me. If you're talking about your daughter—"

"It's not about Kendra. Unless you count that she was the one who made me start thinking about you."

"She finally asked you what happened between us?"

He nodded. "And you were right. Discussing it with her could have poured salt on the wounds of her insecurity. Especially since it came up the night before she left for school."

"Could have?" Thea stared at him. "What did you tell her?"

"Fortunately, I didn't have to say anything. I was saved by the bell."

"I'm going to take a wild guess here and assume you're not talking about me."

"Mike came over to say goodbye to Kendra."

"Okay. But I still don't see—"

"Just stop interrupting and I'll get there faster. Mike said I was an idiot if I let you get away. I should have figured it out for myself, but—" He shrugged. "I didn't."

"Figured what out?"

"That I was looking for an excuse to walk away from you. I've been single for a long time because putting everything on the line, risking it all again, was something I didn't want to do. I didn't want to get burned again."

"And now?"

"You made me want to get burned," he said, heat sparking in his eyes. "I'm ready to take a chance again."

A few weeks ago, the words would have sent her over the moon with happiness. But now she'd managed to stanch her bleeding emotions. She couldn't afford to be a basket case. Not again. Not with the baby coming. She didn't trust this sudden about-face. She refused to have expectations or hope. Most of all, she wouldn't let herself need him. He might be there today and possibly even tomorrow. But what about the long haul? She couldn't let her guard down.

She could only count on herself. Strength was her middle name. Independence was her new best friend.

She looked up at him and a shaft of sunlight caught her in the eye. With a hand on her forehead to shade her gaze, she saw the hope in his expression and steeled herself against it.

"I'm sorry, Scott. I can't take the chance that this change of heart isn't just about Kendra leaving home. You made it clear you don't care enough about me and the baby."

"That's just it. Don't you see? I'm willing to accept the baby."

Her heart twisted at his words. "The problem is, you don't see. I can't be with a man who's 'willing' to 'accept' my child. It's not fair to me, or the baby, or you for that matter. Don't misunderstand, I want this baby to have a father. It breaks my heart that he or she won't have one. But that man needs to be with us because he wants to. We need a man who sees a baby as a blessing, not a burden. And you've made it clear from the first day I met you how you feel about it."

"Thea, listen to me—"

"No."

She stepped to the back of the SUV and started to slide a box toward her from the rear hatch. Scott moved beside her, close enough for her to feel the heat of his body. He reached out and moved her aside.

"You shouldn't be carrying stuff in your condition." His voice was rough yet warm, like sandpaper dipped in whiskey.

Through a blur of tears, she saw the muscles and tendons in his forearm flex with harnessed strength. Not now, she thought. She'd managed to get through everything without dissolving in a puddle of tears and she was awfully proud of herself for that. It hadn't been easy, what with her jam-packed, hormone-ridden body. Now he had to go and do something sweet like this.

"I won't hurt my baby. Now will you please go away? I don't want to see you anymore."

"Too bad." He glared at her. "I'm going to unload the back of this car. If you have a problem with that, don't watch. But if you pick up anything heavier than a throw pillow—"

Thea didn't wait to hear the rest. She couldn't stand this. He was showing her what it should have been like and it was too cruel. It was a glimpse into what might have been—like a peek into heaven when your soul was damned to hell.

She turned on her heel and went inside, upstairs where she could be alone. In her master bedroom, tears trickled down her cheeks while she ripped open boxes. Finally she found the one with the towels. She grabbed one and buried her face in it so he wouldn't hear her sob.

She didn't know how long she cried, but she stayed like that until she had no more tears left. Before going back downstairs, she peeked out the window and saw that his truck was gone.

"I guess I got through to him," she said.

But the thought held no satisfaction, just a mother lode of pain from a broken heart she knew would never heal.

Now who was the idiot who needed a good swift kick in the caboose?

Chapter Sixteen

Scott walked into For Whom the Bell Toils and saw the flowers he'd sent to Thea on her desk, but she was nowhere in sight. And he hadn't seen her SUV outside. It had been a week since they'd made their respective moves. A week since he'd seen the tears in her eyes as she'd turned her back on him. Seven days since he'd watched her stiff back as she'd walked away from him. One hundred and sixty-eight hours during which he'd called and left messages she hadn't returned. He was going out of his mind.

"Hello?" he called out.

Connie appeared in the doorway to the back room. She frowned when she saw him and the look of hostility on her face clearly said what she thought of him. "We've got to get that dinger fixed."

"I don't give a damn about the damn dinger. Where's Thea. I need to talk to her."

Her expression went from hostile to stubborn as she

folded her arms over her chest. "She doesn't want to talk to you."

"She's made that clear. But I've got some things to say to her."

"Don't you get it? She doesn't want to hear any more from you."

"I get it, I just refuse to accept it." He ran his fingers through his hair. "Look, Connie, I know I've made a few mistakes—"

"A few?" she said, one auburn eyebrow going up.

"Okay, a lot. And they're really big mistakes. Whoppers. But I need to explain to her. I've tried sending flowers, calling, leaving messages she doesn't return. I don't know what to do if she won't even talk to me. I need help."

She sighed and moved farther into the room, stopping by Thea's desk. Leaning forward, she breathed in the scent of the blooms. "She loves these lilies. How did you know?"

"I didn't. Just a shot in the dark. But I'm glad. Here's the thing. If I'm going to convince her I'm sincere, I need someone with the inside track. I need to know how to get through to her."

"What if I help you and she never speaks to me again?"

Something in his own chest pulled tight. "If you don't, you'll be responsible for two people missing out on an opportunity for happiness. Thea and I will be miserable for the rest of our lives. And it will be on your head." He watched her face, the emotions shifting there and decided to keep pressing. "You don't have to like me, but this is your chance to be her friend."

"As her friend, I will honor my promise to run interference."

"Is she happy?" When Connie didn't answer, he swore silently. He wished she wasn't fitting the profile of the stubborn redhead. "If you can honestly tell me that she's better off and completely content, I'll back off."

He mentally crossed his fingers and prayed she wouldn't call his bluff.

Connie's forehead creased with doubt. "What if I help you and you break her heart?"

He let out a long breath. "I already did that by being a jerk. She's the best thing that ever happened to me. I need to put her heart back together and spend the rest of my life making it up to her."

"I can't stand to see her so sad," Connie said, and he knew she was relenting. Then she glared and pointed at him. "But if you let her down again, I'm coming after you, buster. And it won't be pretty."

"I won't hurt her, I swear. Now help me. What should I do."

"Court her."

"Tried that," he said, pointing to the bouquet in the vase beside her. "I even sent some to her at the house and she still won't speak to me."

"Flowers, candy," she said, ticking off on her fingers typical courting gestures. "Candy's out. She's watching her weight with the pregnancy. Her motto is anything over twenty-five pounds isn't baby. So food would probably earn you demerits." She looked at him. "You've got your work cut out for you."

"Has she mentioned me at all?"

Connie shook her head. "Thea internalizes everything. I watched her go through David's death and the stages of grief. I've watched her do the same thing with you."

"I'm not dead."

"To her you are. And right now she's working on acceptance. If she gets there—" She shook her head and he didn't want to think about what that meant.

"How do I keep her from getting there?"

"Shake her up. Make promises—preferably ones you intend to keep."

"That's the only kind I make."

She studied him as if she was gauging his sincerity. Whatever she saw seemed to satisfy her because she nodded her head. "Somehow you need to get her off balance."

"How?"

"I haven't got a clue. But it needs to be big. Look, Scott, she got clobbered really bad. The lesson she learned was that if she doesn't let herself care, she won't be hurt again."

"I get that, but—"

She held up her hand. "Let me finish. Now she's got the baby to think about. All of her maternal instincts are on high alert. You turned your back on her because of her baby. She's not likely to give you another chance to hurt her child."

This wasn't making him feel better. "I made a mistake. I admit that, but—"

"I'm not saying you're a bad guy. Look, I've got kids. I know how hard a job it is. And consciously choosing it again is a tough decision."

"No, it's not."

He knew he'd given the correct answer when a small smile curved her mouth. "I'm not the one you have to convince."

"How do I do that? Especially when she won't talk to me."

"My best advice is show up and keep showing up. When you do, speak from the heart and do what you do best."

"That's not especially helpful since I'm just a dad who happens to be a building contractor." He shrugged.

"Then do dad stuff and build something. I don't know what else to tell you. If that doesn't help, you're on your own, pal."

"Can you at least tell me where to find her?"

She shook her head. "She just said she had time between appointments and she was going to check out baby furniture."

"Where?"

"She didn't say. But I know she's planning to furnish the nursery soon."

Scott nodded. "Okay. I appreciate the help, Connie."

"Good luck."

"I'm going to need a miracle," he said, then walked outside.

Glancing up at the sky, he thought about David. He would never see the baby Thea had fought so hard to bring into the world. Would he want another man to be there for her and his child? "If so, now would be a good time for a little divine inspiration."

Thea had been in Scott's house for several weeks when she realized she was still thinking of her new home that way. It was time to stop. Partly because every time she did, there was that annoying empty feeling followed swiftly by a sensation of pressure around her heart. This was *her* house, damn it, and she was going to be happy in it.

But she couldn't stifle her disappointment that he'd

stopped calling and sending flowers. Apparently he'd given up trying to communicate with her, just when she'd been on the verge of giving in. How perverse was that?

But it was for the best, she told herself. Herself replied that it didn't feel best. Loneliness was funny that way.

The timer on the microwave signaled that her frozen dinner was ready at the same time the doorbell rang. She wasn't expecting anyone and was surprised to have company. It was probably Connie. She'd talked about a housewarming gift.

But when she opened the front door, the man standing there didn't look anything like her partner. The man standing there was Scott. Her heart did a happy little dance, proving that all her conditioning to accept their situation had been a waste of perfectly good mental energy.

"Hello, Thea."

He looked good—really, really good. Better than she'd ever seen him. Or was that because she'd missed him so deeply? Or because she hadn't expected to see him again?

"What are you doing here?"

"I have something for you."

She didn't want anything but him. The thought made her work harder at steeling herself against loving him. "I can't accept anything from you."

"Will you at least look at it?"

She couldn't resist the pleading expression in his eyes. Not to mention the pleading in her heart. "Okay."

He nodded and said, "Hold that thought. I'll be right back."

Then he was gone. She heard the microwave timer

beep, reminding her with its relentless, annoying chirp that she hadn't taken her food out. She walked into the kitchen to do that and shut the appliance up. After grabbing a pot holder, she removed the steaming cardboard-encased meal and set it on the island. Then she heard the front door close.

"Thea?"

She went into the living room. Scott stood there and at his feet was a wooden cradle, with the curved runners to make it rock. She'd expected flowers maybe. Or a plant as a housewarming. But this looked like handmade furniture, a fine sturdy piece of wood with two intertwined hearts carved into the headboard and footboard. Her own heart pounded when she realized the significance of a baby's first bed and the intricate carving. She was speechless.

"I made it for the baby," he explained.

She wanted to ask what it meant, absurdly hoping for the moon, the sun and the stars. "Why?" she finally said.

"Because I can." He shrugged.

"Scott, I'm not sure what this is about, but you and I are over—"

He shook his head. "Don't say that. As far as I'm concerned, things between us are just getting started."

Her whole body began to shake. "I don't understand."

"I do. I get that you're afraid to care again. I was, too. But something scared me more."

"What?" she whispered.

"Living without you." A muscle in his jaw moved. "When you walked away from me that day, I got the worst feeling deep in my gut. It got bigger when you wouldn't speak to me or return my calls. Every day that went by, it got worse. Because I love you, Thea."

Her eyes grew moist as she looked at him, making his image waver. She'd longed for and dreaded hearing him say those words.

"It's too late for us, Scott. It can't work." She shook her head. "You've already raised two kids. 'Never again,' you said."

"How come it's a woman's prerogative to change her mind, but a man has to live and die by whatever stupid words come out of his mouth?"

"I don't know," she admitted. "I thought when you stopped calling and sending flowers that—"

"I'd given up?" He shook his head. "I just decided to invest my energy in the future." He stepped closer and took her hands in his. "Thea, this isn't simply a cradle."

"No?" She nudged it with her bare toe and watched it rock. "Looks like it to me."

"It's a symbol. Of my commitment to you and the baby."

"How can I believe you mean what you're saying?"

"Life doesn't come with a guarantee. Sooner or later you're just going to have to take a leap of faith. This is my way of prodding you over the edge. Take a chance, Thea. I'll make sure you don't regret it."

"If only I could be certain—"

Gently but firmly, he squeezed her hands. "I only do two things well. I'm a builder and a father. The cradle I built will keep the baby safe and secure until he outgrows it. The father in me wants to see him grow. I want to build this child with you. I want to make a difference for the better—with you."

The tears gathering in her eyes spilled over her lower lashes and rolled down her cheeks. But her voice was steady when she spoke. "I don't know what to say."

"You've said you want your child to have a father. Someone who sees him as a blessing. I'm your man— a family man."

Her heart swelled to bursting with happiness. Thea could no more turn him away than she could turn her back on the promise she'd made to the other man she'd loved. And somehow she had the absurd feeling that David heartily approved of Scott Matthews. Maybe because she'd found love again and it felt so very right to her.

Scott squeezed the hands he still held. "I mean this with all my heart, Thea. If you'll give me another chance, I'll spend the rest of my life multiplying your happiness and dividing your sorrow."

She smiled through her tears and whispered a single word past the lump in her throat. "Okay."

He pulled her into his arms and drew in a shuddering breath. "Thank God."

She savored the strength and heat of his body to reassure herself that he was real, that this wasn't a dream. "You called the baby 'he.' Do you know something I don't know?"

"Nope. I just couldn't call our baby 'it.'"

The words warmed her as surely as the Sterno flame on a chafing dish. "Well, it's official. I'm head over heels in love with you, Scott Matthews."

When he looked at her, his mouth curved up. "Good. That tips the scale in my favor for the question I'm about to ask."

"Ask away," she said, sniffling.

"Since you're officially in love with me, and I'm officially in love with you, what we need here is an official proposal of marriage." He got down on one knee and lifted a jeweler's box from the cradle. He took her left hand, then slipped the ring on the appropriate finger. "Will you marry me?"

She saw the hope and sincerity in his eyes and had no more doubts. There was only one right answer to his question. "Yes," she said without hesitation.

She borrowed hope from him and transplanted it in her own heart to grow again. For a while, hers had been lost. Not anymore, thanks to Scott.

Epilogue

Scott stared into the cradle he'd made and watched the month-old baby boy squirm and squeak. Glancing at the clock on Thea's side of the bed, he read 2:00 a.m.

"Right on time, T.D.," he whispered, stroking a finger over the infant's perfect head full of downy dark hair. "But your mom could use a little more sleep, so I'm on diaper duty. Maybe I can hold you off just a little bit before she feeds you."

Gently, he lifted the child and carried him into the other bedroom of the house he'd sold to Thea. He chuckled as he thought about the nightmare of paperwork they'd gone through to change the title on this house and the condo into both their names after getting married. Now they rented out the town house and set up a home in the bigger house where he'd raised T.D.'s two sisters.

"Kendra and Gail are coming home tomorrow. Your sisters wouldn't come home for your mom and me, but they can't wait to see you on the weekend," he said to the little guy.

When he was finished changing the baby, he put his hand on the boy's belly and stared in awe at this beautiful child, truly a miracle. Scott was more grateful than he could put into words that Thea had let him into her life. Not only that, she loved him. God knew why, but he was glad she did and wasn't going to question her judgment. He was a lucky man, he thought, remembering the man who would never see his son's face.

"David," he whispered into the night, "I love Thea and this child with all my heart. I'll be the best father I know how to be and guide him with all the wisdom Kendra and Gail gave me. Granted, they're girls, but—"

When he felt a small hand on his back, he looked into his wife's warm brown eyes. At that moment they were suspiciously bright.

"Hi, sweetheart," he said. "Didn't mean to wake you."

"You didn't. I guess it's a mom thing, but I sort of know when Thomas David needs something."

He pointed to her chest. "It couldn't have anything to do with the fact that you're ready to breast-feed T.D.?"

She laughed. "Maybe. And about those initials—"

"It means touchdown," he defended.

"So you've said. But we spent many hours picking an appropriate name for our son."

Scott remembered. They'd teased about Hildegard for a girl or Ichabod for a boy. "And your point?"

"We picked the middle name David for the man who gave him life. And Thomas for the man who gave you life and raised you to be the special man you are."

He leaned down and kissed her nose. "Thank you."

"You're welcome. But if T.D. sticks, all those hours spent agonizing over his name will be a waste of energy."

"And if you insist on calling him Thomas David, he'll get beat up every day after school."

"You're right," she said, sighing.

He blinked. "That easy?"

"It's not easy. It's all about balance. And thank goodness you're here to do that for us. T.D. is very lucky to have you."

"He's more lucky to have you for a mother."

Leaning her cheek against his arm, she put her hand beside his on the baby who was dozing on the changing table.

"You and I are so lucky," she said. "To have such special children. We met thanks to Kendra, who was reaching out for the mother she missed. And now we're raising this little guy who won't have to reach out for a father he doesn't have."

"I'm not perfect," he reminded her, not for the first time.

"Perfection is highly overrated." She gazed up at him. "Do you know why I fell in love with you?"

"No." He couldn't resist asking. "Why?"

"Because you were such a good father to the girls."

"But I made so many mistakes."

"To be sure. In spite of that, you kept trying, doing more right than wrong. I love and admire you more every day."

"Do you know why I fell in love with you?"

"No. Why?"

"Beats the heck out of me," he teased.

She slugged him playfully. "I take back everything nice I said."

"Okay. Seriously. I fell in love with you because you're hot." He braced himself for another assault.

But she stood on tiptoe and kissed his cheek. "That's the nicest thing you could have said to a woman who recently gave birth and has the postpartum body to prove it."

He shook his head. "Not once have you ever done what I expected," he said, shaking his head. "And I really think that's why I fell in love with you."

Gazing up at him, she smiled the sweet smile he loved so much. "It doesn't really matter why. The important thing is that we do."

"Yeah."

"I thought I loved you before, but sharing this child with you, watching the way you care for him, makes me realize the capacity for love is endless and forever."

"Amen," he said. "But I'm not ashamed to admit that I love you because you're hot, too."

The sound of her laughter warmed his heart. As he looked up, he thought of David. A feeling of peace settled over him and he knew all was right in the universe. And he knew his love for this woman was eternal. Just as he knew that Thea Bell Matthews would forever ring his chimes. Once upon a time, he'd thought she was all he needed to be happy. But her special brand of love showed him it takes three.

* * * * *

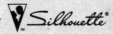

SPECIAL EDITION™

Coming in September 2004
from beloved author

ALLISON LEIGH

Home on the Ranch

(Silhouette Special Edition #1633)

When his daughter suffered a riding
accident, reclusive rancher Cage Buchanan
vowed to do anything to mend his daughter's
broken body and spirit. Even if that promise
meant hiring his enemy's daughter, Belle Day.
And though Cage thought Belle was the last
person he needed in his life, she drew him
like a moth to a flame....

Available at your favorite retail outlet.

SPECIAL EDITION™

Book Three in the exciting saga of

THE PARKS EMPIRE

Dark secrets. Old lies. New loves.

The Rich Man's Son

(Silhouette Special Edition #1634)
Coming in September 2004

from reader favorite

JUDY DUARTE

When angry young Rowan Parks tries to flee his
present after a fight with his father, he ends up in
a bad accident and loses his past—to amnesia!
Unable to recall anything about what he was
running from—or to—he accepts help from beautiful
Louanne Brown, a local rancher and single mom
struggling to make ends meet. What Rowan
doesn't know is that Louanne is also trying to hide
from an evil threat—and as they begin to fall for
each other, the danger puts their future at risk!

Available at your favorite retail outlet.

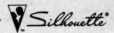

SPECIAL EDITION™

The Baby They Both Loved

by

NIKKI BENJAMIN

(Silhouette Special Edition #1635)

The lure of Simon Gilmore's
masculine strength was almost more
than Kit Davenport could resist.
But as long as he had the right to
take her adopted baby—*his* son—
away from her, he was the enemy....

Wasn't he?

*Available September 2004
at your favorite retail outlet.*

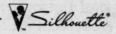

SPECIAL EDITION™

A Texas Tale

by

JUDITH LYONS

(Silhouette Special Edition #1637)

Crissy Albreit was a bona fide risk taker
as part of the daredevil troupe the
Alpine Angels. But Tate McCade was
offering a risk even Crissy wasn't sure
she wanted to take: move to Texas and
run the ranch her good-for-nothing
father left behind after his death. Crissy
long ago said goodbye to her past.
Now this McCade guy came bearing
a key to it? And maybe even one to
her future as well....

*Available September 2004
at your favorite retail outlet.*

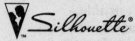

COMING NEXT MONTH

#1633 HOME ON THE RANCH—Allison Leigh
Men of the Double S
Rancher Cage Buchanan would do anything to help his child—
even if it meant enlisting the aid of his enemy's daughter.
Beautiful Belle Day could no more ignore Cage's plea for help
than she could deny the passion that smoldered between them.
But could a long-buried secret undermine the happiness they'd
found in each other's arms?

#1634 THE RICH MAN'S SON—Judy Duarte
The Parks Empire
After prodigal heir Rowan Parks suffered a motorcycle accident,
single mom Luanne Brown took him in and tended to his wounds.
Bridled emotion soon led to unleashed love, but there was one
hitch: he couldn't remember his past—and she couldn't forget
hers....

#1635 THE BABY THEY BOTH LOVED—Nikki Benjamin
When writer Simon Gilmore discovered a son he never knew
was his, he had to fight the child's legal guardian, green-eyed
waitress Kit Davenport, for custody. Initially enemies, soon
Simon and Kit started to see each other in a new light. Would
the baby they both loved lead to one loving family?

#1636 A FATHER'S SACRIFICE—Karen Sandler
After years of battling his darkest demons, Jameson O'Connell
discovered that Nina Russo had mothered his chid. The world-
weary town outcast never forgot the passionate night that they
shared and was determined to be a father to his son...but could
his years of excruciating personal sacrifice finally earn him the
love of his life?

#1637 A TEXAS TALE—Judith Lyons
Rancher Tate McCade's mission was to get Crissy Albreit back
to the ranch her father wanted her to have. Not only did Tate's
brown-eyed assurance tempt Crissy back to the ranch she so
despised, but pretty soon he had her tempted into something
more...to be in his arms forever.

#1638 HER KIND OF COWBOY—Pat Warren
Jesse Calder had left Abby Martin with a promise to return...
but that had been five years ago. Now, the lies between them
may be more than Abby can forgive—even with the spark still
burning. Especially since this single mom is guarding a secret of
her own: a little girl with eyes an all-too-familiar shade of Calder
blue...

SSECNM0804

SPECIAL EDITION